ISBN 9781957864310
EBOOK ISBN 9781957864327

COZY MYSTERY | DARK ACADEMIA

Wild Lark Books
513 Broadway Street
Lubbock, TX 79401
info@wildlarkbooks.com
wildlarkbooks.com

DYING TO DONATE

Support Authors

Will you help support an artist?

Wild Lark Books is an independent publisher that supports authors as artists. As with all works of art, reviews help books be seen by new readers.

Please support this author's artistry by submitting reviews. It would mean the world to us!

shop.wildlarkbooks.com
librarything.com
bookshop.org
goodreads.com

Support Art. Read Books.
Wild Lark Books

Dying to Donate

LAUREN CASSEL BROWNELL

WILD LARK BOOKS

For Jaybird and Suebird

Contents

"No man should escape our universities without knowing how little he knows."

-J. Robert Oppenheimer

Chapter 1

"Harper, we've lost your father."

I was stunned into silence. A lightning-fast stream of memories with my dad rushed through my mind and tears welled up in my eyes. Recovering my voice I said, "Mom, my God. What happened?"

"I went to take a bath. He was watching TV. I got out of the tub, and he was gone."

"Oh Mom. I don't know what to say. What do you need me to do? Do you think...was it...?" I stumbled over my words, unsure of what to ask. I fell back on platitudes I had heard others rely on in times like these. "I guess it's a blessing he went quickly and didn't suffer."

"Harper, what are you talking about? I don't know if he went quickly or slowly. I just know he went."

"What are you talking about?" I asked. My mother sounded confused. "Do you know who you're supposed to call when someone dies?" I was uncertain if, in her state of mind, she would have thought of what to do next.

"Your father isn't dead Harper. He's missing."

"What do you mean he's missing?"

My mother began rambling again about taking her bath and him watching television and how they had spaghetti for dinner. My relief that Daddy wasn't dead was mixed with extreme frustration.

"Have you called the police?" I interrupted.

"No, I haven't called the police. I called you first."

"And what the hell am I supposed to do? I'm 400 miles away. Get off the damn phone and call the police, Mom."

"But what do I tell them?"

"You tell them exactly what you told me. Dad has dementia and he has wandered off. Call them. Now!"

The overwhelming sadness that had swept over me when I thought my father was dead quickly transformed into anger and disbelief that my mother called me before calling the police. I had always thought of my mother as a strong and capable woman. She had been a well-respected businesswoman and a leader in the community. But lately it seemed she reverted to complete helplessness in the midst of any sort of crisis. One day she had called me in a panic because the grocery store was out of distilled water, and that was the kind she needed to put in her humidifier. The smaller the problem, the more unable she seemed to solve it.

One of my defining characteristics that is both a blessing and a curse, is I'm always able to see both sides of a situation. My dad used to say I'd make a great lawyer as I could argue a case for the defense or the prosecution. So, I sat down on my secondhand sofa (I preferred to think of it as vintage), took a deep breath, and considered my options. I could stay put. My mom would call the police and they would take care of the situation. I called my mother's cell phone, and it went straight to voicemail. Good. She must be on the phone to the police. On the other hand, what if things went really wrong? What if they found my father dead in a ditch? No. Surely, they would find him quickly.

And alive. He was a seventy-five-year-old man with dementia. How far could he have gotten?

Struggling to be logical and not let my emotions overwhelm me, I went a few back-and-forths with myself and decided I had no choice but to get to Shepperton as quickly as possible. The story I had been working on would have to wait. It was more important I ensure my father was safe and support my mother.

My story. That's what I had been working on when my mother called. It would be more accurate to say I was procrastinating on working on my story. I had checked email multiple times, opened both Facebook and Twitter, and watered my plants.

I worked for a small magazine along with three other writers and the owner and editor, Allison Summers. I had been freelancing and picking up writing jobs here and there and managing to make ends meet for close to eight years now. The gig with Allison was the closest thing I'd had to a real job although I still didn't have benefits or a retirement plan. I was still young, I told myself, having just turned thirty. I'd worry about retirement later. For now, I could get things settled in Shepperton and still meet my Monday deadline.

Within the hour I was on the interstate headed west.

As the city lights dimmed behind me and the road ahead stretched on with only the occasional car heading the other direction, my mind wandered. How had things gotten to this point? My father had begun the descent into dementia about two years before. It was slow at first—little things forgotten or misplaced, confusion at some activities that had before been commonplace. It coincided with his retirement from the university. As a journalism professor at Murdoch

Collier University, he was vibrant and on top of his game. But once he began spending his days puttering around the house with Mom, his minor slips turned into gaping stumbles.

I tried my mother's phone again. Voicemail. Something felt really wrong. I pushed slightly on the accelerator and set the cruise control to eighty-two, which on the flat Texas highway was a reasonable - if not legal - speed, even in the dark.

About three hours into the six-hour trip, my phone rang, startling me from my reverie. It was the police, letting me know they had found my father. He was disheveled, confused, and had been robbed of his wallet and watch. Thank God he hadn't been killed. They were keeping him in the hospital at least overnight for observation. I told them I was on my way, and they suggested I meet my mother at the hospital.

I felt a sense of enormous relief they had found Dad alive, yet I still felt an overwhelming apprehension as I continued west. I tried to drown out the thoughts with my favorite Spotify playlists and a stale cup of coffee I got when I stopped for gas.

Eventually, after driving for hours across terrain that, during the day, looked eerily similar to pictures taken by the Mars Rover, I took a right off of the interstate and onto the smaller highway I would follow north across the West Texas plains into Shepperton.

Ah, Shepperton. If you blinked, you might miss it. As you come up over a small hill, one of the few in the region, and look into the distance to your left, there sits Shepperton. It is the prettiest town in the notoriously dry and flat West Texas plains. Some unknown (at least to me) geological force caused this one section of the terrain to be populated with rolling hills and able to support the growth of grass and green trees. The town spread out from its shining jewel, the Murdoch Collier University campus.

That campus. The home of many of my fondest childhood memories. That campus. The place that made me feel suffocated by the expectations of others that I would grow up and be like my father, the beloved professor. Once upon a time my father was eccentric. Now he was demented and had been wandering the streets of Shepperton. I shook these thoughts from my head as I pulled into the parking lot of Murdoch Memorial Hospital and took a deep breath to steel myself for whatever was awaiting me.

As the sliding glass doors parted, the universal hospital smell immediately hit me. How do all hospitals on earth have that same smell? Weird, sickly sweet, cleaning fluid combined with...what? Illness? Death? Fear? And I say universal. I really don't know that for certain. I've never been to a hospital in Japan or France, for example. Thus, I can only say for sure that every single hospital I've ever been to in the United States has the same smell. It's sort of like the smell of a Target. Have you ever noticed that every single Target smells exactly the same? It's this kind of stale popcorn smell, but strangely, it makes you want to spend money on things you don't even need.

The next thing I noticed was the lights. The bright white fluorescent lights that take away any ability to judge what time of day it is, what the weather is - anything outside the mini-universe of the hospital. They were blinding after the dark night and headlights of my drive. I blinked and tried to get my bearings. The hospital was surprisingly busy for the early hour but glancing at my phone I realized it was probably getting close to a shift change. Good luck getting any information out of anybody at this hour.

I followed the signs overhead leading me to the emergency room. I had no idea where else to start. The clerk at the check-in desk was eventually able to tell me where my father was after scanning her computer for what seemed like forever. I sighed deeply as I rode the elevator to the third floor. The adrenaline and bad coffee that had gotten me this far were waning, and exhaustion was taking its place.

I pushed the door to room 308E open as quietly as I could, steeling myself for what I would find behind the door. Over the course of a boring six-hour drive your mind can imagine all sorts of horrors. But to my relief, Dad looked great. He was sleeping soundly, his cheeks pink, and no sign of worry furrowing his forehead, which was usually knitted tightly into wrinkles. He was a kind and gregarious man for the most part, but he also spent a great deal of time in deep thought, and this manifested itself in his wrinkled brow.

What I was not prepared for was how bad my mother looked. She was curled up in a ball in a recliner on the far side of the room. As I laid my hand on her shoulder, I noticed several lines on her face that hadn't been there the last time I saw her. When was that exactly? Had it been that long? Or had caring for my father aged her this rapidly? Her body looked small and frail under the light hospital blanket. She stirred and opened her eyes, let out a deep, dry cough, and looked up at me. The circles under her eyes were a deep purple and, her eyes were bloodshot., and she still seemed confused.

"Harper? Is that you?"

"I'm here, Mom. How's Daddy?"

"You shouldn't have come all this way. You don't have time for this. Don't you need to be at work?"

"Mom, stop. I have plenty of time. Always enough time for you and Dad." She smiled and patted my hand.

My dad's feet moved under the covers, and I stepped towards his bedside.

"Daddy? It's Harper. I'm here."

"Did you bring breakfast?" he asked without opening his eyes. I chuckled, thinking he was being funny. But it quickly dawned on me as he opened his eyes and looked at me blankly, it wasn't a joke at all. He didn't know who I was and thought I was a hospital worker bringing breakfast.

"Did you bring breakfast?" he repeated loudly. "I don't want any of the crap you served me yesterday." He attempted to push himself up in the bed and I tried to wrap my arms around him to help him.

"Don't you touch me. I do not like to be manhandled by the help."

I started to explain I wasn't the help but stopped myself. I had read enough about dementia to know arguing with him would most likely agitate him further and elevate my stress level, which was already off the charts. My eyes stung with tears. I turned back to my mother who had closed her eyes again and was shaking her head gently back and forth.

"Mom?"

It was one questioning word, but it held within it so many unknowns. How and when had Dad gone so dramatically downhill? Was my mom's health failing or was she exhausted from a terrible night? Why hadn't she been honest with me? Told me how bad things had gotten? And the biggest question of all racing through my mind—if she had told me, would I even have listened?

Chapter 2

I made the choice to leave Shepperton a long time ago. Yes, there was the weight of expectations, but there was so much more to it. I had felt stifled by life in Shepperton—like I couldn't be myself. Everyone in town knew my parents and had certain ideas about how things should be, and who I should be. How could I be free to live my life and make my own mistakes under the ever-watchful eye of an entire town? My dad was somewhat of a public figure and people thought my life was up for scrutiny as well. If I made even the slightest mistake, it was public knowledge and I always felt judged. Every time I drove into town, seeing the Shepperton city limit sign made me claustrophobic. The expectations pressed against the windshield and the car windows as I drove into town. I couldn't breathe. And I could hear the phrases people repeated over and over and over again whenever they ran into me.

"Are you going to be a professor like your father?"

"Must be nice to have a career waiting for you."

"The Fox legacy—alive and well at MCU."

I wanted no part of it. I stayed at MCU only long enough to get my diploma, hand it to my parents, load my suitcase in my car, and get the hell out of town. I traveled a little on money I had saved waiting tables at Mustang's, one of the few restaurants in the area back then, and then took a string of writing jobs at various small publications. Eventually I settled in Dallas and found my current writing gig. Yes, as much as I had wanted to separate myself from my dad's looming persona as a former award-winning journalist and journalism professor, I became a writer.

I think there was a part of me that loved the idea of the romanticized part of journalism. My dad would tell me stories about his travels and stories he had covered. It sounded exotic and exciting. When I would ask him why he gave it all up, he would always say, "Because I wanted to marry your mother more." Apparently, Mom said she wouldn't marry my father if he continued to travel all the time and volunteer for every assignment that took place in a militarized zone. I thought it was a crappy ultimatum, but I suppose it worked out for them.

I had once asked them what brought them to Shepperton of all places, as neither of them had grown up in the area. I was surprised by their answer. They had intended to buy *The Shepperton Sentinel*, the local newspaper. Mom had a background in advertising and was going to run the business side of the paper while Dad continued his journalistic passions, at a slower and less dangerous pace. When I asked what happened, they changed the subject quickly saying only that the deal fell through. I knew instinctively the topic was not open for discussion.

My dad had managed to earn a master's degree between writing assignments and, fortunately I guess, this, coupled with his real-world experience, was adequate enough for him to get hired to teach undergrad journalism courses at MCU until he and my mother decided what to do next. But next never came. Dad pursued a PhD, and my mom turned her sites on the one advertising agency in town. Starting as a junior copy assistant, she worked her way up the ladder until, by the time I was in high school, she was a managing partner. It seemed life had worked out well for my parents, but I couldn't help but feel it was not truly the life they had wanted or envisioned for themselves. They came to Shepperton with a dream and by default, they never left.

I was determined not to let the same thing happen to me. I would not get sucked into a life in Shepperton based on complacency. It broke my heart that this powerhouse of a woman now panicked over a lack of distilled water at the grocery store.

At that moment, a nurse popped in and distracted me from my musings.

"How are we this morning?" she asked to no one in particular.

"We want our damn breakfast," my father replied. "But not the same crap as yesterday."

"Oh Frank, you know you weren't even here for breakfast yesterday," the nurse laughed as she moved efficiently around my dad, checking his vital signs. She seemed totally oblivious to my presence, which was fine with me. It was strange to hear her referring to my father by his first name. Even I often referred to him as Professor Fox. It was who he was.

"It looks like we are going to keep you another night, hon. Since it's the weekend and you had such a big night last night, they want to run a few tests they can't run until to-morrow." The nurse continued to talk directly to my father, completely ignoring my mother and me.

"Get out of the way of the TV," Dad bellowed at her. "I'm trying to watch the game." The small television hanging in the corner of the hospital room wasn't on. We all fell silent as the nurse continued her ministrations. This loud, bossy, mean spirited man was not the father I knew.

"Well," I said eventually, uncomfortable with the silence. "Why don't I run to the house and freshen up while Dad has breakfast. Mama, what do you need me to bring you from the house?"

My mother moved more quickly than I had seen in years as she jumped from the recliner. "No, Harper! You stay here with your dad and visit. I'll go get what we need from the house."

"It looks like you could use some rest, Mom. Stay here and relax."

Honestly, I was still trying to process what I had found upon my arrival. here. I needed to get out of the hospital and think through the situation a bit. And I didn't want to be left alone with my dad not knowing how he would respond to me.

"I'll bring you a breakfast tray. Helen, is it?" the nurse inquired, finally speaking warmly to my mother. "You and Frank can enjoy a nice breakfast together. I'll keep an eye on them." The nurse winked in my direction.

"Okay. That settles it. What do you need from the house, Mom?"

My mom looked defeated as she sat back down in the recliner. "Nothing. Maybe a clean pair of pajamas for your father."

I retraced my steps out of the hospital only getting lost twice in the labyrinth of halls that all looked exactly the same. As I exited the hospital, the constant West Texas wind was refreshing. But one thought kept running through my mind. I had expected to find my dad out of sorts, but why was my mom behaving so strangely?

The first sign something was not right at my parents' house was the front yard. Always my mom's pride and joy, the grass was in dead patches in some places and over-grown in others. The perennials in the beds had been left to wither and die. Even the potted geraniums on the front porch were dead. Yes, it was October, but in Texas we often had to keep our yards tended until almost Thanksgiving. I had never seen the yard look this...abandoned. The con-dition of the yard, however, did not prepare me for what I found as I entered my childhood home.

I used the keys on my keyring to unlock first the screen door and then another key to unlock the heavy wooden door. The house smelled musty and sour. Simultaneously I noticed how dark it was. All the curtains were drawn com-pletely and not a ray of what was now midmorning light shone through. I continued to make my way through the house trying to process what I was seeing. Dishes were piled in the kitchen sink. Stacks of papers, pamphlets, and un-opened mail covered the dining table. For a brief moment I tried to justify the mess with the fact a major emergency had occurred the night before. But in reality, that in no way explained the condition of the house. No wonder my mother hadn't wanted me to come. As I wandered through the house, my anxiety level continued to rise, and a new emotion emerged. Guilt. How long had I stayed away? Eigh-teen months? Two years?

I began my search for pajamas in my parents' bed-room. I then looked in the dryer in the laundry room off the kitchen. Nothing. I continued down the hallway to the guest room which had obviously become my dad's room.

There was a hospital bed where a set of twin beds had been. What the hell? I finally found a pair of pajamas in a chest of drawers and tucked them in my bag still hanging from my shoulder. I had been so shocked by the condition of the house I hadn't even set my bag down when I came in.

I talked to my mom at least once a week and she always insisted everything was fine. I was trying to build my career. They understood. But also, perhaps, I wasn't really listening. It dawned on me I never talked to my dad during those brief weekly phone calls. Had I turned my back on my parents? Was I partly to blame for this situation? *Nothing quite like the guilt of an only child*, I thought.

I walked into the guest bathroom thinking Dad might need some toiletries. The first thing I noticed was the handicapped shower chair in the bathtub. A metal railing had been installed along the wall, obviously providing support to stand and move around the bathroom. A fresh new wave of exhaustion swept over me as I looked at myself in the harsh bathroom lights.

My mousy-brown roots were in sharp contrast to the L'oreal strawberry-blond ends of my hair. I pinched the sallow skin of my cheeks trying to bring my face back to life. It was an exercise in futility. I looked terrible.

But I had to keep moving forward. I filed all my fears and concerns away as I compartmentalized the situation. I needed to wrap things up here quickly and get back to Dallas by noon tomorrow. I threw a toothbrush and a razor into my bag with the pajamas and headed back to the hospital.

***

"Mom, we need to talk."

"Not now, Harper. Your father just fell asleep."

I pulled up an extra chair and took my mom's hands in mine.

"What is this?" I asked.

Mom had a device attached to her finger with a wire extending from it.

"It's nothing." She pulled her hand back quickly.

The nurse had appeared again. Damn, she was quiet.

"Your mom had a little low blood pressure episode. She was feeling faint, and we wanted to make sure she was okay. That's a pulse oximeter. It's checking to see she's getting enough oxygen." The nurse looked at the digital readout. "Ninety-four. Not bad, but I'd like it to be a little better. Relax and take some slow deep breaths."

"Mom. You need help taking care of Dad. And obviously taking care of yourself as well."

"I'm fine, Harper. Things are fine."

"Clearly things are not fine. You need..."

A knock on the door interrupted my train of thought, and before I could continue, the door was already swinging open, revealing a face that was almost as familiar as my own.

"They said I could find you here, but I had to see it for myself," said the handsome man peeking around the doorway.

"All the rumors are true!" I smiled, rising from the chair and crossing the room to hug my dear, old friend Matt Langley. "You look wonderful, Matt. How long has it been?"

Somehow, seeing Matt's face suddenly brought the reality of the situation home to me and I found myself overwhelmed by the events of the last few hours. I fell into his arms. His hug felt like safety, like melancholy, like sentimentality. And he still smelled the same as he had in high school. Like soap. And youth. It momentarily drowned out the hospital smell.

Matt and I had been best friends from middle school all the way to our sophomore year of college. I can't remember exactly why we drifted apart then, but at the moment, it didn't matter. I was so glad to see a familiar face.

Matt returned my hug and then held me away from him, looking at me as if in disbelief I was standing in front of him. "It's been at least five years. Is that even possible?"

"I heard you've been busy these past five years. Is the rumor true I now have to call you Doctor Langley?"

"Yep. I am a newly minted Assistant Professor of Marketing and Communication at MCU. The lowliest rung on the academic ladder. But at least I'm climbing."

"Hello Dr. Langley." My mom had pulled the pulse ox from her finger and kissed Matt's cheek as she moved towards the door. "I'm going to the cafeteria for a cup of coffee."

We watched her departure and I turned back to Matt. "Wow. I am so proud of you. My dad would be so proud of you." I glanced over my shoulder at his sleeping figure.

"How is he doing?" Matt asked.

"Wait. How did you even know he was here? How did you know I was here?"

"You know how fast news travels in this town. I knew you were coming before you even hit the city limits."

"I do not miss that aspect of life in Shepperton."

"But you have missed me, haven't you?"

"Maybe a little, every so often." I couldn't help but smile again, even though the weight of the world was on my shoulders.

"Let's get out of here. Let me buy you a cup of coffee. I'll give you a tour around town and we can catch up!" Matt's eyes twinkled in that sweet way they always had.

"I really can't. Somebody needs to stay here with Dad."

"Nope. Frank needs to get some rest," the nurse interjected in our conversation. "Go have coffee with this handsome gentleman. I've got things covered here."

"But I told my mom I would..."

"Go," said the nurse.

"Come on. One coffee," Matt wheedled.

"Let me take a raincheck. I'm exhausted and won't be very good company anyway."

"Fine. But do not leave town until we get to catch up. You always leave before I ever get a chance to see you!"

Guilty. The few times I had returned to Shepperton over the last few years, I was in and out before I had a chance to see anyone but my parents.

"I promise."

Matt kissed the top of my head, glanced at my sleeping father, and left the room quietly.

I took a deep breath and was pondering taking a nap on the room's built-in vinyl sofa when another knock sounded on the door. Matt had always had a way of taking several attempts to leave. He would forget his phone or remember one more thing he had to tell me. It's funny how details you hadn't thought about in ages came rushing back.

"What did you forget?" I said, pulling open the heavy hospital door. But it wasn't Matt. It was a guy I'd never seen before with a camera hanging around his neck, and he was in my dad's hospital room before I knew it.

"I'm Nate Stinton. I'm the editor in chief of the *MCU Mirror* and I need a quote about your dad's condition."

As quickly as he burst into the room, I was equally as quick in grabbing the back of his shirt and pushing and pulling him back towards the door.

"We have no comment. How the hell did you even know my father was in the hospital? Get out! Who let you in here?" Acting purely on adrenaline shooting through my veins, my words were a jumbled mess as they tumbled from my mouth. Getting increasingly louder I repeated, "Get out!"

"Ms. Fox...you are Harper Fox, his daughter, right? Ms. Fox, this is big news for MCU. A beloved professor wandering the streets of Shepperton in his pajamas? I owe it to my readers..."

"Oh please. You don't owe your readers shit. Get out! And if I see one word of this in print, I will sue you for both libel and slander!" I was now pushing him with all my strength, but the wiry little reporter was equally determined not to be forced from the room.

"This is neither libelous nor slander. I'm simply covering a story important to MCU."

"Not today you aren't. I'm about to call security."

"Fine. I'll go. But here's my card. Call me when you'd like to talk about this!"

The young man fished in his pocket and handed me a crumpled business card I ripped from his hand and shoved into my own pocket. "Don't hold your breath boy reporter. Out!" One final push and he was across the threshold. I closed the door quickly and firmly behind him. I was out of breath and sure my blood pressure was off the charts. Heeding the advice the nurse had given my mother, I took some slow deep breaths.

My dad's dementia was now the stuff of university news?

"Who the hell was that?" my father grumbled from his bed.

"Nobody, Daddy. Don't worry about it."

"That's all anybody ever says to me anymore. Don't worry. I'll damn well worry if I want to." He closed his eyes and was back asleep and breathing softly almost immediately.

I had expected this trip would be a challenge, but at the moment, the challenges seemed to be increasing by the minute.

Chapter 3

Mom and I had stayed up into the wee hours that night debating what to do about Daddy. She was in complete denial he needed full-time care and insisted she could care for him at home. She used to be reasonable.

"Mom, I don't want to upset you any further, but you have to understand. This has gotten beyond what you can do alone. You weren't even able to take a bath without him wandering off. And I'm sure this isn't the first issue you've had. You haven't been being honest with me. The house is a wreck..."

"Now Harper, I have been working on getting the house organized. I got a little behind."

"Mom, you're more than a little behind. And I know you don't want to hear this either, but I'm worried about your health. You can care-give yourself into an early grave if you're not careful."

My arguments were ignored. She insisted no one else would understand his eccentricities or be able to reason with him the way she could. She knew how to manage his care. The night of his disappearance was a fluke, she insisted, and must have been her fault. She had obviously forgotten to lock both doors and it wouldn't happen again. I couldn't make her see reason and we kept going round and round. I even tried arguing how much it would ease my stress not to worry about them every day. There was no convincing her.

"We are not a problem you need to solve, Harper."

"No, I didn't mean it like that."

"We are grown adults and we can handle this ourselves. There's no need for you to be worried."

"But I am worried, Mom. You need to know what your options are."

She paused. "I guess it wouldn't hurt to get some information. But only information. And only at Castle Woods."

All I knew about Castle Woods was it was an old folk's home located on the edge of campus. I had some friends when I was in school that were nursing students and they had taken classes there. No one knew why the facility was named Castle Woods, as it neither looked like a castle nor were there any woods within a hundred miles. But as long as it had existed, that was what it was always called.

For my mom to give even an inch and allow me to inquire about Castle Woods was a small victory, but it was a start. I kissed her goodnight, got ready for bed, pulled my laptop open, and started to Google.

Castle Woods was, from all reports, an outstanding facility and one of the few geriatric teaching facilities in the area. The website touted its affiliation with MCU's gerontology department and how it provided state-of-the-art care and an opportunity for research into dementia and related conditions by MCU faculty. It also served as a training ground for affiliated health care careers. Based on everything I read, reviews from the family members of current and former patients, and the cheerful photos populating their website, I could certainly live with Dad being at Castle Woods.

Knowing you couldn't always trust marketing information, I searched on a bit further looking for any news items about Castle Woods. Everything seemed positive and there was nothing particularly newsworthy until I found a blurb about MCU administration engaging in talks with an outside corporation, AgeStage, about buying the facility. The blurb was from two years ago. Apparently, nothing further had come from the discussions. Interesting. I wondered why the university would even consider selling.

Oh well, not my problem. My problem was finding the right place for my dad and convincing my mom he needed to be there. I closed my computer and drifted off into an uneasy sleep.

***

I arrived at Castle Woods early Monday morning feeling somewhat optimistic. Ten years ago this building had been isolated on the northernmost edge of campus, but in the years since I had been away, apartment buildings had sprung up around it to provide housing for the growing student population. Castle Woods no longer sat alone, but it still had a large green lawn in front and a circular drive leading to its main entrance. Big rustic rocking chairs sat on the front patio next to beautiful pots of plants. The lobby was decorated in traditional southwestern decor and felt warm and welcoming. I walked with false confidence towards the woman at the reception desk, wondering what the facility looked like behind the double hospital-like doors that led off the lobby into the rest of the facility.

"I'd like to see the director please," I announced.

"I'm Annette Smith. Executive Director here at Castle Woods." The stern-looking woman had bleached hair pulled back in a bun so tightly it stretched her face taught. She had put strong emphasis on the words executive director, and I must have looked at her questioningly as she quickly explained, "We are extremely short staffed. That's why I'm at the front desk."

"Oh, of course," I nodded. I instantly disliked the woman, but I had to be my most charming in order to accomplish my goal.

"Ms. Smith, I find myself in need of a new home for my father, Dr. Frank Fox. I know Castle Woods is the best facility in the area, and I need to explore your opportunities."

"I'm sorry, Ms....?"

"Fox."

"Ms. Fox. I'm deeply sorry but we have no space available."

"What do you mean you have no space available?" Looking back, I'm not sure how, but I had never even considered this possibility.

"We are currently at one hundred percent capacity. We have no openings available. You are welcome to place your father on our waiting list. I expect we might have some openings in six months or so."

"Six months? I need to know what my options are now. But...but...we can't wait. He needs someplace now. They are releasing my father from the hospital this afternoon. My mother is overwhelmed with his care..."

"Sadly, it is a story we hear often. Our services are in very high demand. Our strategic marketing initiatives as well as very positive word of mouth in the community, have assured we stay almost completely occupied at all times. We don't have any beds right now. Nor do I anticipate us having any openings in the near future." She said the last sentence as if I was stupid and might not have understood what she was saying. Smith sounded like she was repeating verbatim the text I had read on the website the night before. It was slick and used all the buzzwords, much like Annette Smith herself.

"I don't care about your strategic marketing initiatives, Ms. Smith. I care about my father. He was an esteemed professor at this university for decades."

"So are most of the other potential candidates on our waitlist, I'm afraid. It is the clientele we serve, and we strive and succeed to meet our quotas." More jargon.

"What do you suggest I do?" I struggled to keep sarcasm out of my tone.

"I suggest you review your father's benefits and look at other facilities in the area that could accommodate your needs."

"Anyplace you would suggest?"

"Oh dear, no. The care at Castle Woods is unparalleled in this region."

Tears stung my eyes as I gave the unpleasant and completely unsympathetic woman my contact information. I'd made a few baby steps with my mother and now I was back at ground zero. I'd have to try and convince her to consider other options. "Please call me the minute anything becomes available."

She gave me a curt nod and turned towards what I assumed to be her office behind the front counter.

"Thanks for nothing," I muttered under my breath as I walked out the front door.

I was not going to let Annette Smith see it, but I was devastated. Castle Woods had been my only hope. I would take my mom on a tour, explain the relationship with MCU and she would see it was a perfect solution. What was I going to do now? I was completely naïve in thinking I could make these arrangements this morning and be on my way back to Dallas. But God only knows how long my father could be on the waiting list. What would I do in the meantime? After seeing the condition of my mother, my father, and their house, I knew I couldn't leave. At least not today.

While walking to my car, my phone rang. I fished it out of the bottom of the enormous bag I always carried. It held everything I thought I might ever need and then some.

"Hey Allison," I said to my boss from *Dallas Alice Magazine.* "How are you?"

"I am waiting for your story. That's how I am."

Crap!

"I am so, so sorry. I forgot to call. My dad was hospitalized over the weekend, and I had to make an emergency trip home. I will have it for you by noon tomorrow. I promise."

"Fine." The line went dead.

I wanted to break down and cry, go find my mom, and pull the covers over my head. However, I had discovered long ago that was no way to get things done. What was the next logical move? I took a deep breath.

The next best step was clearly to follow Annette Smith's advice and go to the Human Resource office on campus to find out what my father's benefit package would cover. Then I would have an idea of what I was working with.

I had been skirting around the edges of campus almost as if I was afraid to get too close ever since I arrived in town. A trip to HR would require me to go right into the middle of it. Parking was a nightmare, as always, but I figured a walk might help me clear my mind. After circling the commuter lot for what seemed like half an hour, I followed a student to their car in the farthest row and pulled in quickly before anyone else saw it.

Does a college campus exist that has enough parking? If so, I've never heard of it. Even back when I was at MCU you could never find a parking spot. And the student body had literally grown by thousands since then. Everybody I knew that worked at or attended a university had the same complaint, regardless of their role or the size of their campus. I had a sneaking suspicion colleges made more off of parking tickets than tuition.

Another person looking for parking honked at me aggressively. It seemed they had been eyeing the same spot. I waved innocently and began the hike towards the main building. With its pink granite facade, gray arching accent stones, and ivy climbing its walls, it oozed academia. I wondered how they managed to grow ivy in the West Texas heat.

As I entered the building, my shoes clicked on the marble floor. I made my way up the center stairs that branched off towards opposite wings on the second floor. From the few times I had been in this building, if I remembered correctly, the human resource office was to the left, but as I moved down the hallway, all the carved wooden doors looked identical and, my luck, none of them were marked.

I walked slowly down the hallway trying to find some indicator of what lay beyond the doors, but realizing I was wasting valuable time, I pushed one open at random. Twenty sets of eyeballs turned towards me as I interrupted a class in session.

"Can I help you?" said the professor from his lectern in a tone dripping with sarcasm.

"I'm...um... looking for Human Resources," I squeaked. How could a college professor, any college professor, intimidate me this way? It was yet another thing I hated about this place.

The professor rolled his eyes and sighed heavily. "Back down the hallway to the third door on your right. Or...maybe it's the fourth."

"Thank you. Sorry to interrupt."

I backed out of the door quickly and proceeded back down the hallway the way I came, counting doors. Was it the third or the fourth? I twisted the brass knob and pushed open the third door that opened into what was clearly not human resources. It was a beautifully appointed sitting area. Two overstuffed royal blue sofas sat on each side of an intricately carved coffee table that was as large as my entire apartment in Dallas. Magazines fanned out on the table along with various university propaganda...I mean, marketing brochures. On the other side of the room was a large cherrywood desk behind which sat a mature and well-coiffed woman who was staring intently at her screen. She finally turned her eyes towards me and said, "May I help you, dear?"

"Yes ma'am," I said, moving into the beautiful room. "I'm lost and looking for..."

Before I could finish my request for directions, the interior door flew open and hit the wall with a loud bang that made both me and the woman jump. In the doorway stood a tall man made even taller by the cowboy boots he was wearing. I probably wouldn't have noticed them (I mean, lots of people wear cowboy boots out here) had they not been a bright shade of turquoise. His face was bright red, and he was sweating profusely. "I'm not gonna stand for this!" he shouted over his shoulder into the office from which he had come.

"I'm sorry you feel that way, Steve. I truly am," came a far calmer voice from within the inner sanctum.

"You damn well will be sorry, you son of a bitch." The booted man stormed past me and threw upon the door into the hallway. You could hear his boots hitting the marble floor heavily as he stormed down the hallway and down the stairs. For a moment, a vacuum was left in his wake.

"Oh my," the woman behind the desk finally said under her breath.

The man attached to the calm voice emerged from the office and I quickly recognized him as university president Dr. Wells. "No need to fret, Sheila. Just another great meeting with Dr. Ryan."

It was only then he noticed me and smiled warmly.

"I didn't realize we had company." He walked towards me with his hand extended. "I'm Joe Wells, president here at MCU."

He was completely unphased by the scene that had unfolded even though I was still shaky from the slamming doors, raised voices, and threats, but I extended my hand as well and said, "I'm looking for Human Resources."

He laughed. "You wouldn't believe how many people come in here looking for HR. Sheila, when are we going to get those nameplates put up?" Then he looked at me closely. "Have we met before? You look awfully familiar."

"Yes. I was a student here several years ago. And my father is a...was a professor here. I'm Harper Fox."

"Harper Fox...of course! I was so sorry to hear about your dad but thank goodness they found him so quickly."

Oh great, I thought. News of my father's middle of the night outdoor excursion had made it all the way up the ladder to the president's office. "Yes. We were very relieved," I said. "Now, um...Human Resources?"

"Right next door," Sheila chimed.

President Wells patted me on the shoulder and said, "You give your mother my regards and if there is anything we can do for you, anything at all, you let me know."

It took all my strength not to blurt out, "Get my dad a room at Castle Woods!" But I couldn't. This was something I had to deal with on my own. It was against everything I stood for to use the good will of the university president to help my father. It was a lesson my dad had instilled in me. "You must stand on your own two feet," he would say. "You can't rely on other people to do for you what you can do for yourself." I had learned the lesson very well, being almost obsessive about never asking for help.

After finally finding Human Resources (actually the fifth door on the right), I realized doing it on my own was going to be damn near impossible.

"I'm sorry dear, but we cannot give you any information about your father's university benefits."

"And why is that?" I again had to watch my tone.

"You aren't listed as next of kin or beneficiary. I'm afraid I can only provide information to your mother. I assume Helen Fox is your mother?" At least the woman in HR was nice about it, unlike Annette Smith at Castle Woods.

"Yes, that's my mother and she's got a husband in the hospital suffering from dementia. She's got her hands full." I thought this approach might work better because the truth was getting me nowhere. "She asked me to come over here today to get this information. We need to know what his options are for care." My mom would kill me if she knew I was here, but what she didn't know wouldn't hurt her.

"I would recommend you look at Castle Woods. It is by far the best facility in the area and many of our retirees find..."

"Yes," I interrupted. "I've already been to Castle Woods. They have no space available for my father, and I need to know my options. Today!"

It was as if I could hear the time ticking in my head. My father was being released from the hospital in a matter of hours and I had no idea what I was going to do.

"I am only allowed to give information to your mother. Unless you have paperwork showing they have given you your father's power of attorney, I'm afraid I can't do anything for you."

"And how do I get that?" There it was in the distance. A dim glimmer of hope.

"You need a lawyer who is familiar with your family's situation. They can draw up those papers for you. It usually takes about two weeks to get everything processed."

And the glimmer was doused. Two weeks. I barely had two hours to find a place for my dad and convince my mother to take advantage of it. Tears stung my eyes again and I turned away before the woman could see my weakness. My trip to Old Main was a total bust and I had nothing to show for it except more roadblocks.

I was lost in thought and mumbling to myself as I descended the staircase, running headfirst into someone coming up the stairs using the same banister. "I'm sorry! I wasn't looking ...Oh, it's you."

"Have you reconsidered giving me an exclusive on your dad, Ms. Fox?"

"Absolutely not," I replied sharply, brushing by what's his name. All I could think of was Jimmy Olsen, but I knew that wasn't right. "No comment!" I threw back over my shoulder.

I hiked the mile back to my car swearing I would never go to campus again. As I approached, I could see a yellow piece of paper tucked under my windshield wiper. An MCU parking violation. I snatched the ticket and cursed loudly. Once I was in the car and had turned on the air conditioning, I sat there. What was I going to do now? I hate not being in control of a situation. I want to act, not sit around and overthink things. But it felt like every direction I turned these days I was facing a dead end.

***

Chapter 4

"When the going gets tough, the tough have coffee. Meet me at Royale on the Square at two," Matt said when I called to tell him about all the obstacles standing between me and getting my father into a memory care facility. I clearly wasn't getting anything else accomplished. I might as well catch up with my friend.

I felt better almost instantly when I saw him standing outside waiting for me. Nothing like old friends. I had missed him. We hugged and I complimented him on his MCU hoodie. "Go Mustangs," I laughed.

"We need to get you some MCU gear. Come with me."

"I need coffee!" I protested.

"Nope, you need an MCU sweatshirt first."

He took my hand and pulled me with him several doors down from the coffee shop to a store called The Magic Mustang. As we entered, I saw it was awash with blue and gold, MCU's school colors. The last thing I wanted was MCU swag, but Matt insisted. He pulled t-shirts, baseball jerseys, and sweatshirts from the racks, holding each one up to me. He even put a baseball cap on my head, destroying any semblance of a hairdo I had.

"Nope, not for you. No, not quite right," he said. I had to laugh. "Oh, now, this...this is the one." He held up a royal-blue sweatshirt that read "Murdoch Collier University —the other MCU" in bright yellow letters.

"I don't get it," I said. "What does that mean? The other MCU?"

"MCU? Marvel Cinematic Universe?"

I shook my head, having no idea what he was talking about.

"Have you been living under a rock? MCU. Spider Man? Iron Man? The Avengers?"

"Nope."

"Oh my gosh. Movie night. ASAP. We've got to get you back among the living. But for now, you need this sweatshirt. It's hilarious. Trust me on this one."

Matt insisted on buying me the sweatshirt, and I told him I would wear it proudly, even though I didn't get the joke.

"And now, coffee." He was grinning from ear to ear as he handed me the bag and we headed back towards Royale.

As we entered the coffee shop, Matt was greeted by the barista. "Where have you been, stranger? You too good for us now you're a doctor? We only see you for catering gigs."

"Yeah. I don't have time to hang around with riff-raff like you anymore," Matt laughed. He pointed me towards a table and said, "I'll get our coffee."

"Matt, you bought me a fifty-dollar sweatshirt. I can get my own coffee," I said.

"Nope. You're a guest. And I still remember how you like it." He spoke to the guy at the counter in hushed tones for a moment before joining me.

"You must have spent a lot of time here while you were in school," I commented.

"Actually I worked here. I needed some way to pay for my PhD as MCU didn't see fit to offer me a fellowship. Royale was my home away from home."

"Here you go, Dr. Langley." A cute blonde, emphasizing the word doctor, delivered our coffees and gave Matt a wink. "Let me know if you need anything else."

"You obviously made a good impression," I said with a smile.

We relaxed back into our chairs and sipped our coffee amiably.

"It has been the weirdest day," I finally said with a sigh.

"Tell me about it," Matt agreed. It was then I noticed he looked tired. Maybe not tired. Worried? Even though my time in Shepperton was limited, I was glad we had decided to meet for coffee. Apparently, we both needed someone to talk to.

"Okay. You first," I said, taking another sip from my delicious coffee, indeed made exactly the way I like it.

"You sure?" he asked.

"Absolutely. Spill it," I replied.

"Okay. So about eleven this morning, I'm sitting at my desk, minding my own business, doing some grading. The dean comes storming into our suite bellowing for everybody to meet in the conference room...immediately."

"Yikes," I said, kind of enjoying not thinking about my own problems for a minute.

"Right? So, everybody drops what they're doing and scurries into the conference room where he starts ranting and raving about fundraising and taking donors to dinner and stuff. I mean, he's wound pretty tight all the time and he's intense. But this was like next level stuff. He starts telling us if we don't bring in funds other than research money, 'changes will have to be made.' He said it just like that. 'Changes will have to be made.' And I swear, he looked right at me."

"What did everybody do?"

"Newer faculty, like me, excused themselves to go throw up..."

"Matt, I'm serious."

"I'm serious too! I've got two other colleagues who were brought on board at the same time as me and we're all sitting in the conference room seeing the writing on the wall. We're junior faculty. First in, first out. Fewer tenure track lines to have to fund. The tenured faculty barely even paid attention. They know he can't do anything to them."

"Geez, who is this guy?"

"Dr. Steve Ryan. I've heard he was some sort of corporate marketing guy before he decided to jump into higher ed and..."

"Did you say Ryan? Steve Ryan is your dean?"

"Yeah. Why?"

"That's part of my weird day. I saw him. Today in the president's office. Dr. Ryan. And he was furious."

"What were you doing in the president's office?"

"You're focusing on the wrong part of the story. Wells and Ryan. They were having a huge fight. And it was right before eleven. He said to the president 'you'll be sorry' or something like that and stormed out of the office. I wonder if this is what they were fighting about?"

"Probably. Times are tough in the old university fundraising world. But I guarantee you everyone in the College of Media and Communication was updating their CV after that. It was weird." Matt sat quietly for a minute, looking as if he was replaying the event in his head. Then he shook it off and smiled.

"Now your turn," he said. "I want to hear about the life of my best friend, the glamorous music journalist."

I paused, caught off-guard. "Um...what makes you think I'm a music journalist?"

"I assumed. Your mom said you were working for a magazine called *Dallas Alice* and your office was in Deep Ellum."

I gave him a puzzled look, unable to see the connection.

"That song by the band Little Feat? 'Oh my pretty Alice, Dallas Alice'." He attempted to hum but I didn't recognize the tune. "Dixie Chicken?"

"Now, I have heard that one."

"I thought ...I guess I thought you were writing for a music magazine. Deep Ellum is kind of the heart of the Dallas music scene, right?"

"Well, kind of the fringe music scene. But that's not the only kind of business located there." I hated to burst his bubble and was honestly kind of embarrassed to tell him the truth. The offices of the magazine I had been writing for were located in Deep Ellum, yes, but it was about as far away from *Rolling Stone* as you could get. Why couldn't he have kept his illusion? But he'd find out eventually. "*Dallas Alice* is a parenting magazine. My boss, Allison, has a three-year-old daughter, Alice. *Dallas Alice.*"

"But you're not a parent," Matt pointed out, as if it was a revelation to me.

"No, but I'm a great writer. And great writers can write about anything, right?" Matt nodded. "The article I am currently working on is about..." I took a deep breath. "...breast pumps for working mothers." There. I'd said it.

Time stopped for a moment. Finally, Matt said, "Well, that's important," and we both burst out laughing.

Changing the subject as quickly as I could, I gave Matt a more detailed update on all the various issues I had encountered in trying to get some help for my dad.

Matt listened intently, as he always had. I knew in his mind he was trying to solve the problem for me and present me with a solution.

"Can you hire home health care to go to the house, care for your dad, and help your mom out?" he asked.

"I thought of that, but apparently the cost is astronomical, and I don't know if my parent's insurance will cover it. Plus, Mom says she would need to get the house in order before she has anybody come in. God only knows how long that could take."

"Okay. What about another facility? I'm sure there are other great places in the area."

"Mom won't even consider another facility. To her it's Castle Woods or bust. It's as if because it's affiliated with MCU it has some sort of Good Housekeeping seal of approval. I'd argue the point, but everybody I've spoken to recommends Castle Woods as well. It's like it's the only game in town."

Matt was obviously as stumped as I was. Finally, he said, "I know this isn't optimal, but could you take FMLA and stay here for a while to smooth the transition?"

I knew he was trying to help, but I was growing more frustrated as I went through these options for the umpteenth time, and my response was edgy and snappish. "Right. Like the crappy parenting magazine I work for has Family Medical Leave Act benefits. I'm lucky I get paid."

"Okay. Okay." Matt held his hands up in mock surrender.

"I'm sorry. I shouldn't be taking this out on you. There has to be something we aren't thinking of."

My phone buzzed in my pocket. "Hang on a second. It's a local number. I better get this," I said. "Hello?"

"Ms. Fox, this is Annette Smith, Executive Director at Castle Woods. We met this morning?"

"Yes, Annette, I remember." I rolled my eyes and Matt laughed.

"We have an unexpected vacancy," she said flatly.

"I...how? Who?" I was clearly at a loss for words.

"If you can get me all the paperwork and your father here by close of business today, the room is yours. If not, it will be going to the next name on the waiting list."

"We'll be there. Thank you, Annette. Thank you so much." My mind was suddenly racing. "Matt, I'm sorry. I've got to go."

"What happened?"

"They have a room at Castle Woods for my father."

"That's great!"

"I have to get him admitted tonight."

"Let me help you!"

"No, I can handle it."

* * *

I was wishing I had taken Matt up on his offer to help as I staggered into Castle Woods under the weight of my father's suitcases. I was already exhausted from the full-scale sales pitch I'd had to give my mother to get her to agree to this move.

"Harper, I'm not ready," she had argued.

"Mom, this chance may not come again. Castle Woods is in high demand. They told me you usually have to wait six months for a room."

"A six month wait would be fine. It would give me time to get my affairs in order and get your father used to this idea."

"And what are you going to do for six months? Tie Daddy to a chair so he doesn't wander off again?"

"Harper, there is no need to be ugly."

"I'm not being ugly. I'm being honest. This is the right thing to do. For both of you."

The only way I had finally convinced her to move forward with Dad's admission to Castle Woods was to promise her we would do what they call a respite stay - a temporary trial run of the facilities if you will.

"Just give it a month. One month! And if you aren't happy, or if he's not happy, we will find another option."

I could see she was considering this, and I had to sit quietly, waiting for her to process the information. Pushing too hard at this moment would cause her to panic and pull the plug entirely on this idea.

"Fine," she finally said. "One month."

With those words, I sprang into action and with warp speed gathered a few of my dad's personal things and got a bag packed. Our next stop was the hospital. In quickly reviewing his discharge orders with the nurse, it struck me as ironic that all of his test results had come back almost perfect. His aging body was in excellent shape. It was his mind that was betraying him.

Going directly from the hospital to Castle Woods had brought out the worst in my dad. I could only imagine how confused he must be by all of this. He sat in his wheel-chair cursing and asking everybody what the hell was going on. With all my mom's attention focused on him, all of my attention was focused on single handedly carrying his suit-cases and the damn end table my mom had insisted we bring to his second-floor room.

My mother was pointlessly asking my father which draw-ers he wanted his things put in and her nervous chatter was driving me up the wall. I excused myself and went down-stairs to find Annette Smith and complete the required paperwork.

Annette was drinking coffee out of her Royale coffee mug and seemed in no great hurry to be of any assistance to me. In fact, she seemed to take some sort of perverse joy in telling me, yet again, I had no legal right to execute any of the paperwork.

"Annette, can you just cut me some slack here? How about I take the paperwork upstairs and let my mom fill it out and bring it back down to you?"

"I'm sorry, Ms. Fox. That is not our procedure here. Please have your mother come down and fill out the required paperwork."

I returned to Dad's room, tired and frustrated, and sent my mother downstairs. I bustled around the room putting things away and saying over and over under my breath, "Everything is fine." Was I saying it to myself or to my father?

A wave of exhaustion swept over me, and I sat down on the edge of the twin bed. A deep sigh escaped my lips.

"Harper baby. Why so pensive?"

Harper baby. That's what he always called me. And pen-sive. What a great word. Leave it to my dad to come up with the right word even in the strangest of situations. He had always been obsessed with building up his own vocabulary—and mine. Summertime during my childhood I would awaken to a list of ten new vocabulary words each day. I had to define them, use them in a written sentence, and sprinkle them throughout dinner conversation that night. At the time I had hated it, but now I could play a mean game of Scrabble, and it was probably my extensive vocabulary that helped make writing enjoyable. Pensive.

As I sat next to him in his new "home" at Castle Woods, I on the edge of the bed and he in his wheelchair, he reached his hand out to me. I took it and we sat in silence for a moment. A rare thunderstorm was brewing, and the wind was whipping through the leaves on the tree outside his window as the sky darkened.

"Dad, I want you to know how much I love you. I know I haven't been around much lately, but I do love you and I thank you for being a good daddy."

"I know, Harper. I love you baby, and I'm so sorry."

"Sorry for what, Daddy?"

"For leaving you."

The door flew open (could no one gently open a door anymore?) and the brief spell was broken by my mother's artificial cheerfulness. We spent a few minutes doing what we could to make the room comfortable and then left my dad for his first night alone at Castle Woods.

* * *

Physically and emotionally drained by the events of the last couple of days, I settled into bed in my parents' guest bedroom. The afternoon had been such a whirlwind I hadn't really been able to process any of it. My body was tired and achy, but my mind was still moving a thousand miles a minute.

How had there been a six-month waiting list at Castle Woods this morning and a room available this afternoon? What was Annette Smith's problem? Accepting the fact I wasn't going to be getting any sleep anytime soon, I turned the light back on and pulled out my laptop. I might as well get the story finished. I had my quotes and research organized in a file on my desktop, ready to be referenced. I clicked it open and perused the notes I had made.

I couldn't focus. My mind kept returning to the most troubling question of all. It was obvious the essence of my dad was still in there somewhere. Why was it so difficult to access?

Chapter 5

Also unable to sleep, Hank Sharp sat up in his bed in his small room at Castle Woods Retirement Village. He swung his legs over the side and placed his feet inside his slippers, as he had done every morning for the last fifty-two years. But was it morning? It was still dark outside.

"I need a glass of milk." Hank spoke to no one in particular. "Maybe Marguerite left me a glass of milk in the refrigerator." He had no idea who Marguerite was or why she would have left milk in the refrigerator for him, but it felt right to say.

He shuffled down the hallways towards the kitchen. Oh, where the hell was the kitchen anyway? Maybe down these stairs?

He felt a hand on his back.

"Marguerite?"

Chapter 6

I finished the story and hit send around two a.m. and tossed and turned for what was left of the night. I was relieved when the digital clock by my bed read a respectable 5:30 so I could get up, get dressed, and start the day. I had worried about Dad all night, certain we had been in such a rush there must be loose ends to tie up. I wanted to get to Castle Woods early.

I have always been a morning person and the early morning hours in West Texas are particularly satisfying. The heat of the day hasn't taken over yet and usually a cool breeze is blowing. Additionally, the doctor on call at Castle Woods the night before had informed me patients were usually at their most lucid in the morning. And the sunrises. Whatever else I thought about this place I was from, nothing quite compared to the sunrises and sunsets of West Texas.

I was marveling at the blues and reds streaking the morning sky, but as I came around the corner, I was quickly brought back to reality as the colors of the sky melded with blue and red flashing lights outside of Castle Woods.

"Daddy!" was the only word in my mind as I squealed into a parking place, jumped from my car, and ran towards the front doors. I was moving much faster than the automatic sliding doors and almost pulled one off its tracks as I burst into the lobby.

"What's going on? Is my dad all right?"

A couple of police officers were milling around the lobby along with members of the night staff, but no one would answer my questions. An employee I had seen last night passed by and I grabbed her arm. "What's going on?" I repeated, my heart in my throat.

"They found Mr. Sharp's body at the bottom of the stairs in the southeast wing this morning. Tragic."

I bent over with my hands on my knees to catch my breath and let the adrenaline slow its coursing through my body. As sad as I was someone lost their life, the relief it wasn't my father was overwhelming.

Once I caught my breath, I wanted to get to my dad as quickly as possible, but the staircase was blocked with yellow and black Caution tape. I headed towards the elevator. On the second floor, I turned left towards 242, the room assigned to my father. After the scene in the lobby, it was strangely quiet. All the doors were closed except for 246. I glanced at the name plate outside. Hank Sharp. My curiosity got the best of me, and I pushed softly on the open door.

The room appeared dark and empty. But then, out of the corner of my eye, I noticed a man standing in the dark, staring out the window. I cleared my throat so as not to startle him, but he didn't respond.

"Excuse me?" I said softly.

The man turned slowly towards me. "I'm sorry. I was a million miles away."

"Oh no...I'm sorry...I'm...um...I'm Harper Fox. My dad is two doors down. I'm...um..." What possible reason could I give for disturbing him? I'm incredibly nosey? I tried to back away, feeling like a total jerk.

"Of course. Come in," he said. *Too late to get away*, I thought. "I'm packing a few things. This was my dad's room. He's moving out. Permanently." He chuckled.

"Um..." I was at a loss for words.

"I'm sorry. That was inappropriate. I always make bad jokes at the worst possible times. I'm David. David Sharp." He moved towards me with his hand outstretched and I took it.

"I heard about your dad. I'm so very sorry for your loss."

He moved towards the bedside table and turned on the lamp, shedding a little soft light onto the room. His face was handsome, and his eyes were dry I noticed. No tears were being shed here.

"No need to be sorry. We weren't that close anymore." He returned to pulling books off a shelf and placing them in a cardboard box sitting on the bed.

"But still..." I said.

He paused, pulling what I could see was an MCU coffee mug off of the shelf. He stared at it for what seemed like an eternity before he continued to speak. "The only thing he cared about was his beloved Murdoch Collier University. He gave them all his time, all his money. He was consumed by it. There was nothing left for us."

I was more uncomfortable by the second. "I'm sorry," I finally whispered. "I'm going to leave you alone to...um...finish your packing."

As I backed out of the room, I could have sworn I heard him say under his breath, "I'm glad he's dead."

* * *

Chapter 7

With things happening so quickly, it seemed only right to stay in Shepperton for at least a few more days. I could spend some time with my dad and help Mom at least start getting the house in order. Wednesday morning, however, got off to a rocky start.

"I told you Castle Woods was no place for your father," my mom said before I'd even had my first cup of coffee.

"What are you talking about? He's been there for one day."

"If Hank Sharp can fall down the stairs, God only knows what could happen to Frank."

"Mom, what happened to Mr. Sharp was an accident. Just a tragic accident. It doesn't have anything to do with Daddy."

"Well, I don't like it. He shouldn't be there."

I knew she was struggling. I had forced her hand in admitting Dad to Castle Woods and it was going to take time to adjust. And as much I hated to admit it, Hank Sharp's fall hadn't exactly made me feel great about the safety of the place either. I bit my tongue and changed the subject. "What can I do for you, Mom? I thought I might get out of the house for a bit. How about I pick up some groceries for us and then we can go visit Daddy this afternoon?"

"There's plenty in there to eat," she said.

I pulled open the refrigerator door and found a container of expired milk, some fat free cottage cheese, and a cantaloupe. "There's nothing in here to eat. I'll stop at the store."

"No, don't waste money until we have time to make a list. I can do it later."

"One of the reasons I'm here is to give you a break from running yourself ragged. Let me do these things for you. Please."

"Well, if you're going out you can stop at the pharmacy. I've got a prescription ready for pickup. Why don't I get my sweater and I'll go with you?"

"I'd really rather you get some rest."

"Fine. I'll sit here like a little old lady and wither away to nothing."

"Okay, Mom. You do that." I grabbed my keys, poured a cup of coffee to-go, and was out the door before any more passive/aggressiveness could occur. I was in need of some space.

That was me, always in need of my own space. I was fifty-fifty a people person and a complete loner. I enjoyed my own company but also felt energized by time around other people. Unfortunately, time with my mom felt draining right now and I needed a break.

Based on experience, I could only assume running errands in Shepperton would be far from the break I needed and it would reinforce how glad I was not to live there. I could see it now. Everywhere I would go I'd run into somebody who had known me growing up or knew my parents. I'd have to give a full explanation of my father's situation at least a dozen times. Even worse, I'd have to answer the "Harper Fox, where have you been?" question two dozen times. Why couldn't people in small towns mind their own business? Or do what we did in big cities—avoid eye contact?

Preparing myself for a bad day, the first thing I needed to do was touch base with Allison. I called her from my cell as I drove towards the Square.

"This article draft you sent in? It's...um...not up to your usual standards, Harper," Allison said once we had been connected. "It's requiring far too much editing and I don't pay you to have to rewrite your work."

"Well, I...I've been distracted I admit. But it wasn't..." I spluttered.

"Are you planning on being back at work soon?" she asked.

"I needed to talk to you about that. I need to stay here for a few more days with my parents and..."

Allison cut me off mid-sentence. "I think it might be best if you take a little leave of absence. It's obvious your head's not in the game. And I don't have time to babysit my writers. I'll edit this piece and get the November issue out without you. Call me when you're ready to refocus."

I was insisting a leave of absence wasn't necessary and I could be back in the office on Monday when I realized I was talking to dead air. "That bitch hung up on me," I said aloud, even though there was no one there to hear me. Allison had always been a bit challenging to work for, but this was ridiculous. "Fine. I didn't need your crummy parenting magazine and stupid breast pump articles anyway."

The reality was I did need her crummy parenting magazine and stupid breast pump articles to pay my bills. I needed this gig and would have to get it together and get back in Allison's good graces. As irritated as I was at the moment, I knew my only option was to take a few more days here in Shepperton and be at my desk at *Dallas Alice* on Monday morning, refocused and ready to start anew. I had a few interesting ideas for the Holiday Gift Guide for Toddlers that might be fun to research. *Or it might be like pulling teeth without anesthesia,* I thought.

I arrived at the square incredulous my mom still insisted on using the drugstore there she'd been using forever. Why not use the big chain store out by the highway? But as I pulled into a parking spot in front of Gage Drugs, I resolved to enjoy being out of the house and enjoy the beautiful day. It was already warm even though it was a mid-October morning, but a breeze blew and made it very pleasant. The sky was intensely blue. These were the things I would focus on.

As I walked inside, I noted Gage's still had a soda fountain along one wall. It brought back memories of cokes and ice cream in this very spot through my childhood and teenage years. It was as if time stood still. As I made my way towards the pharmacy counter in the back, I heard a voice say, "Harper Fox. Is that you?"

At first my stomach dropped at the phrase I dreaded as I looked through the plastic partition to see an old high school classmate. Kyle Baxter had been a total jock in high school, but he had gone against the stereotype by also being kind and sticking up for the underdog. He would never allow anyone to be bullied if he was around, and he acted like everyone he knew was a close friend. I smiled, a genuinely happy smile to see this guy I hadn't thought of in years. He was one of the good guys.

"How are you? Long time no see," he said, coming down the three steps from his podium where prescription drugs were dispensed.

"I'm great. Just in town for a couple of days. It's really great to see you, Kyle." We hugged awkwardly.

"How's your mom? I've been kind of worried about her."

"Unfortunately, it's my dad who is really causing me concern these days. We've admitted him to Castle Woods."

"I am so sorry to hear that. I lost my mom to dementia last year. Heartbreaking."

"Yes, yes, it is." I really had nothing else to say to him, so I stood at the counter, awkwardly shifting my weight from one foot to the other until I finally said, "I guess I better pick up my mom's prescription."

"Oh sure, yes, of course. Let me grab those for you." Kyle sorted through the alphabetized containers behind the counter and pulled out several bags. He handed me four separate prescriptions.

"My mom only said she needed one prescription."

"I noticed she was almost due for refills on those others and went ahead and filled them for her."

"What are all of these?"

"She has one anti-inflammatory. Typical for a woman of her age. To deal with the aches and pains, ya know."

I nodded, even though I didn't know.

"The others are for high blood pressure, cholesterol, and that last one is an additional beta blocker. It slows down your adrenaline when you're under a lot of stress."

"I had no idea my mom was on all these medications. She never said anything to me about it."

"I know things have been tough with your dad lately. I tell a lot of my customers who are caring for a loved one that they have to take care of themselves first. Pull down the old oxygen mask from the airplane and put it on their faces first, ya know."

"But...we were at the hospital with my dad the other day and they said her blood pressure was too low. Is that possible?"

"It might be time for her to visit her doctor and get her meds adjusted. She really needs to be staying on top of her own health these days."

"Okay. I'll let her know. Kyle, thanks for your help today. I really appreciate it."

"Anytime. That's what I love about life in Shepperton. Everybody looks out for everybody else. Don't be a stranger, Harper."

I walked out of the pharmacy feeling mixed emotions. It really had been great to see Kyle, but I now had an entirely new set of concerns. Was my mom keeping health issues of her own a secret? I didn't want to get back in my car and go back to my mom's house, so I turned right and walked down the sidewalk, not even thinking about where I was going until one of the windows of the storefronts facing the square caught my eye. It was fun and colorful with plants hanging everywhere and a display of vintage beauty products and appliances in the huge front window. I took a step back so I could read the name of the business painted in a beautiful font. Rock, Paper, Scissors Hair Studio. Clever. I was intrigued. And in desperate need of a trim.

As I pulled open the door and stepped inside, a bell rang, indicating my arrival. A wave of cool, incense-laden air wafted over me. It reminded me of getting into a swimming pool for the first time each summer—refreshing after a long, cold winter. I closed my eyes and breathed in the smell and tried to capture the moment to return to later. A voice from somewhere in the back called, "Welcome to Rock, Paper, Scissors. Come on in. I'll be right there."

Tristan Miller, yet another acquaintance of mine from high school, emerged from the back. "Harper Fox. My God it has been years," she said, coming towards me with her arms outstretched for a hug. I didn't really like to hug, but somehow Tristan made it impossible not to return the gesture. "Welcome to my little slice of heaven."

"Have you got time for a trim?" I asked.

"How about some color too? I've got time. I had a cancellation."

"Oh no thanks, Tristan. Just a trim. I don't need any color."

"Trust me, Harper. You need color. You'll feel like a new woman."

I glanced at my watch. I didn't have any place to be until my mom and I went to visit Dad later this afternoon.

"What the hell," I acquiesced.

Tristan and I spent the next hour and a half talking nonstop as she snipped and trimmed and placed large pieces of foil in my hair.

"You remember when we had the mysterious lights around here that we thought were UFOs?" Tristan asked.

"Yes! That was like in what? Third grade? Everybody went nuts thinking Shepperton was being invaded."

"If UFOs are anywhere nearby, you should be able to pick up their signals with these," she pointed to the highlighting foils and laughed.

Her laugh was easy and genuine. And her salon was the same way. It appealed to all my senses, and I realized at one point I had forgotten I was in Shepperton. Her salon could have been anywhere in the world. I felt transported.

If someone had told me I'd happily be spending time with Tristan Miller while in Shepperton, I'd have called them a liar. But much to my surprise, the conversation flowed freely, as did the wine she made available to all her clients. We spent a few minutes reminiscing about the "good ol' days," but most of our time together we talked about current events, music (including the great playlist she had on in the background), and her plans for expanding the Rock, Paper, Scissors brand.

"I want to create an entire line of the best quality, all-natural hair care products and sell them exclusively in top salons. I may even open a second location. I'm not sure about that yet."

"Wow, you've got big plans!"

"Oh, I do. Time to rinse." She began peeling the metallic sheets from my hair. "You wanna know what I'm most excited about?"

"Yes!" Her enthusiasm was infectious, and I found I was caught up in her excitement and her vision for the future. "Can I have another glass of wine first?" The sweet blush wine had taken the edge off my frazzled nerves, and I was so relaxed, I couldn't help but ask for a refill.

She poured, continued peeling the aluminum foil from my hair, and said, "This summer, I am going to add 'gallery' to my name and start featuring local artists here. I already have three lined up. They will each have their art on display for a month and we will have a wine and cheese reception for each of the artists to coincide with the summer concert series they have on the courthouse lawn."

"That sounds amazing. I would totally come to that!"

"You are now officially on the invitation list. You'll have to come back for it this summer."

Tristan leaned my head back into the rinsing bowl and applied a delicious smelling mint deep conditioner. When was the last time I had even had so much as a haircut at Great Clips? I couldn't remember. This was decadent.

Once I was completely rinsed, she moved me back to her chair and turned me away from the mirror. She looked at my head thoughtfully, stepping back and moving forward. Clipping a piece here and moving a piece there. Stepping back again and putting a finger to her chin in thought. Finally, she began to blow my hair dry, applying wonderful smelling spritzes of product as she dried.

When she finally turned me around to look at myself in the mirror, I was astonished. "I see why you want a gallery, Tristan. You are an artist!"

"See, I told you you needed some color."

I left the salon with a spring in my step and a promise to be back for the gallery opening in June. It was a promise that even as I said it, I knew I wouldn't keep. While I did feel rejuvenated by the time spent in the salon, reality came crashing back quickly, and something else was bothering me. Something I couldn't quite put my finger on. As I pondered, it occurred to me I felt a sadness for the two former friends I had run into that morning.

Hadn't Kyle Baxter planned on leaving Shepperton and going to medical school? And Tristan? She always said she was going to take the art world by storm. And yet, here they both were, in this little one-horse town, having fallen far short of the dreams they had dreamed while students at Shepperton High School. Thank goodness that hadn't happened to me. I'd gotten out. Gotten away.

Away to what? A job writing articles about breast pumps for a parenting magazine? Saturday nights watering my plants? How was my life so much better than the ones Kyle and Tristan were living? I realized I was doing exactly what I hated others doing to me. I was comparing. I was judging. I was classifying them based on what they had said they thought they wanted when they were eighteen. Kyle appeared genuinely happy about being able to help people in his community. Tristan made this corner of the world beautiful every single day and had big plans for bringing art and culture to this corner of the world. Who was I to judge their paths? It was an eye-opening revelation. Perhaps I had it wrong all along.

Long buried memories came flooding back to me. The way Kyle had always been organizing a fundraiser for a worthy cause or trying to find a home for a stray dog he had found, even when he was a teenager. Tristan had opened her home before events like Homecoming dances or proms to do everyone's hair. Even then she had an eye for style and wanted everyone to look their best. I had only gone to one of her hair house parties, the day of our senior prom. Matt had been my date that year as both of us were between relationships. But with the vanity only an eighteen-year-old can muster, I still wanted to look spectacular. I mean, you only have one senior prom. Tristan had worked her magic on everyone that showed up that day, and I could remember the feeling of camaraderie and joy as we all laughed and listened to music. Those were good times. Why had I only been focusing on the negative memories of life here?

Glancing in a glass store front as I walked around the square back towards my car, I liked the way I looked. And after running into these two long-forgotten friends, I liked the way I felt. Kyle and Tristan were making a difference in their own ways and seemed genuinely happy. I smiled at myself in the glass and let my shoulders relax from where they had been permanently scrunched up around my ears with tension. Even before the fateful call from my mom, I had been uptight and carrying the weight of the world on those shoulders. Maybe it was time to let the burden go.

Back at my car, I glanced at my watch and found I still had a little time before I needed to head home. I dropped the prescriptions in the front seat of my car, walked back into Gage's, and ordered a Rocky Road ice cream cone from the teenager at the soda fountain. Kyle was on the phone but gave me a wave, a smile, and a thumbs up, pointing to my hair. I waved back and stepped out onto the sidewalk.

Since I'd gotten to town, I had been perpetually connected to my phone or walking around with my head hung low in worry. I was going to take a moment and enjoy myself. I licked around the edge of the cone to catch the drips and started around the square again, at a far more leisurely pace.

As in many small Texas towns, Shepperton's downtown square was built around the courthouse, a beautiful building with intricate detailing and well-maintained lawns, dotted with statues of local war heroes. The square was the centerpiece for several businesses owned by people unwilling to be put out of business by the Walmart that opened on the outskirts of town (like Gage Drugs), or visionaries who wanted to be a part of a downtown revitalization and renaissance (like Tristan's Rock, Paper, Scissors).

As I meandered, I thought back to an article I had written about courthouse culture for a Texas travel magazine. I glanced over and admired the grounds. Texas was one of a select few states where the design and construction of the courthouse and the surrounding town square was a competitive sport - particularly among small-town politicians at the turn of the century. Incredibly beautiful architecture can still be found in small cities across the Texas countryside with a wide variety of establishments around it, along with highways leading off from it to the next town. Each courthouse square I had researched looked almost as if a set designer had been hired to create the picturesque scenes.

Shepperton was once a hub for commerce in the region with its train station and central location. Thus, it also served as the county seat of Murdoch County. This dual role ensured that our courthouse was particularly big and beautiful. A gazebo graced the courthouse grounds where local politicians once grandstanded. They were now used for live music festivals on hot Friday nights in summer, just as Tristan had mentioned.

Next to Gage's was a hardware store where you could get both customer service and any part you needed for any type of repair. Royale Coffee sat on the corner with bistro tables outside for enjoying a latte and the fall weather. Catty corner from Royale were the offices of *The Shepperton Sentinel*. I really should ask my mom what had happened with that. Surely enough time had passed and she would be more forthcoming with information. How different might our lives have been if they had taken it over all those years ago?

I continued on past The Magic Mustang, reminding myself to look up the Marvel Cinematic Universe when I had the chance, and then passed the brightly decorated windows of Pei King. They had been a welcome addition to the square back when I was in college and had become a hot spot for takeout. I passed Rock, Paper, Scissors again and peeked through the window intending to wave at Tristan, but she was engrossed with another client, so I continued my stroll. A cute gift shop had taken over the space that used to be a dry cleaner, and a law office occupied the two-story building on yet another corner. A bookstore had moved into the old bank building, and I made a mental note to come back and explore it if time allowed. All in all, a lovely little town square. You could find almost everything you needed right here, or at least pass a pleasant afternoon.

It was time to get back to reality, but for the first time in a long time I felt refreshed. Maybe I could handle this situation. And maybe, just maybe, I was learning a thing or two about myself in the process.

***

I picked up my mother and we headed to Castle Woods where we arrived to find a Bingo tournament in full swing. My dad was in his wheelchair in a far corner of the room and my mother quickly moved him to a table and set up cards for both of them. A table was set up in the back with refreshments and I helped myself to a cup of coffee from a silver urn poured into a Royale coffee cup. I picked up a chocolate chip cookie as my mom called out, "Bingo!" She won a Castle Woods tote bag and was as thrilled as if she had won a new car.

Dinner was served at four thirty, so mom and I stayed to have dinner with Daddy in the cafeteria. What they touted as gourmet dining was...not. My father refused to eat, and I picked at my plate. Tension was returning to my shoulders as I tried to hold on to the pleasantness of the day, but it was difficult. After returning Daddy to his room, Mom and I went home, made a little awkward small talk, and went to bed early.

I spent most of the next day at Castle Woods with Daddy. Mom said she wasn't feeling well, but I was certain the emotional toll of recent events had taken a toll on her. I wanted to talk about the multiple medications I had discovered she was taking but felt like now was not the time for a confrontation. A peaceful day with no acrimony would do us both good. I was also hoping if I was able to spend some time alone with my dad, maybe we could reconnect like we had for that brief moment the night he moved in.

It was funny even with dementia, my dad could beat me at Trivial Pursuit. In reality, it wasn't funny at all. It was a bit frustrating. And humbling. Often, he couldn't remember my name, yet he could tell you quickly which British Sunday newspaper published the first crossword puzzle in 1924 (The Express), or that Louise Brown was the world's first test tube baby.

"You win again, Dad."

"Where's your mother?"

"She's at the house."

"Why can't I be at the house?"

"Because you need to be here for now, Daddy." I wanted to cry.

"It's about time to go," he said.

* * *

By Friday, Mom finally had her grocery list together and off we went to the Piggly Wiggly (yes, that is really the name of the grocery store). At one point I looked down and noticed she had more cottage cheese and cantaloupe in her cart.

"Mom, you can't live on cottage cheese alone."

"I happen to like cottage cheese. It's high protein and low fat. You eat what you want, and I'll eat what I want." What I wanted was five packages of double stuffed Oreos, but I knew that wouldn't solve anything.

While sorting through the milk cartons trying to find one with the latest expiration date, I heard my mother say in her artificial southern belle tone she adopted when trying to impress someone, "As I live and breathe. It has been too long. I have been praying for your family."

"I appreciate that Mrs. Fox," said a deep male voice that rang a tiny bell of familiarity. "It's been tough, but we're going to be fine."

A sideways glance revealed what I had suspected. It was him. The creepy guy from Hank Sharp's room. Oh, what was his name?

"David, I don't believe you've met my daughter. Harper, this is David Sharp."

I was standing there awkwardly with a gallon jug of two percent milk in my hands. "Um...yes... we've met."

"And I am so sorry about that strange encounter," David said with a smile. "I think I was in a bit of shock. Harper came by Dad's room when I was cleaning it out right after..." he was explaining this to my mother, who was nodding sympathetically.

They made small talk for a few minutes about people I didn't know or care about and finally we went our separate ways to finish our shopping. As we got in the car my mother said, "That David Sharp is a nice young man. Why didn't you tell me you had met him before?"

"It's hardly like we met, Mom. His dad had been found dead in a stairwell and he was cleaning out his room."

"You know," my mom said conspiratorially, "Hank Sharp wasn't really David's dad. He was his grandfather. David's parents were killed in a car accident when he was a boy, and Hank and Marguerite raised those children as their own. It was a tragic time for Shepperton."

"That is sad," was all I could think of to say as I started the car and headed towards the house.

***

I had been having trouble sleeping ever since I had arrived in Shepperton, whether it was from not being in my own bed or worrying about my parents. But finally, as Friday rolled into Saturday, I was getting some much-needed rest. Of course, that was also when my mom decided to rejoin the living and act like her old self.

"Why are you still in bed? It's time to go," she said, throwing open the bedroom door.

"Go where?" I said, pulling a pillow over my head.

"To Hank Sharp's funeral. We're leaving in ten minutes."

There was the woman I knew and loved, always on the go with somewhere to be. I also knew, from the tone of her voice, she meant business. I slipped on the one dress I had packed, pulled my hair up in a bun, and wandered into the living room looking for my shoes.

As I tried to shove an earring into my ear without the aid of a mirror I said, "Are you sure you want to go to this service? Why can't we stay home and watch a movie or something? You've been dealing with a lot lately. No one would blame you if you didn't go."

"You sound like you're the little old lady here," she replied, coming around the corner from the hallway dressed to the nines. She looked beautiful and vibrant. The mom I remembered. "Get in the car. Hank Sharp was an important man in this town. We need to pay our respects."

Funerals were certainly not a favorite pastime, but I was particularly leery of running into David Sharp again. The incident at Castle Woods when I first encountered him had given me a case of the creeps I was having trouble shaking, and seeing him again at the grocery store had done nothing to soothe my unease. But as I saw the look on my mother's face, I knew it was pointless to argue with her.

"Fine." I slipped on my shoes and headed towards the car.

* * *

Of course, my mother was right. The service for Henry Bartholomew Sharp was one of the biggest events Shepperton had seen in recent memory. At least that's what I heard two ladies in front of me say as we were waiting to sign the guest book.

"I haven't seen a turnout like this at a funeral in years," said the woman in the dark purple dress and matching hat.

"I know it. I wish Marguerite could have seen this turnout," replied her companion, wearing a lovely navy-blue suit.

I felt self-conscious and completely underdressed for what was apparently the social event of the season. Community leaders, university administrators, and an overflow of townspeople, each one identified to me by my mother pointing and whispering in my ear, lined the pews of the First Methodist Church of Shepperton.

I was relieved to see Matt winding his way through the crowd towards us as Mother and I searched for seats. He motioned for us to join him in a section reserved for faculty.

The service went on for what seemed like an eternity and when I thought it was almost over, the minister asked people to rise from their seats and make their way to the front of the chapel to share a memory or funny anecdote. Apparently, he threw a "helluva tailgate party" and "bled blue and gold." As the stories continued, I was getting antsy and fidgeting in my seat, crossing my legs first one way and then the other trying to get comfortable.

"Stop acting like a three-year-old. Sit still!" my mother chastised.

At long last the minister called the congregation back to order. *Thank God this is over,* I thought. Instead, he said, "For our final speaker of the day..."

My moan was audible, and people nearby turned to stare. Next to me, Matt tried to suppress a giggle.

".... I want to introduce a man who is no stranger to most of you, nor was he a stranger to Mr. Sharp. I am pleased to introduce Murdoch Collier University's Vice President of Development, Dr. David Sharp."

I snapped to attention. I hadn't noticed him sitting in the front row with the other university administrators. As he made his way up to the podium to speak, my mind was reeling.

He cleared his throat. "We are here today to honor a great man," he began. "A man who had an unwavering passion for this university. And a man who had the foresight and vision to ensure his legacy would live on long after he passed from this earth. I am pleased to announce Henry Bartholomew Sharp has bequeathed ten million dollars to ensure the naming rights for the MCU College of Media and Communication. Congratulations to Dr. Steve Ryan, Dean of the College. Come on up here and join me, Steve."

The applause was thunderous and the hamster wheel in my head was about to spin off its tracks. I glanced over at Matt and could see he too was trying to process what was happening. What I thought was supposed to be a day of mourning had turned into a day of celebration for a huge contribution to the MCU coffers. The "mourners" were still on their feet and cheering the news of this gift. And the dead man's son? Or grandson as I now knew. The one I was certain had said he was glad the man was dead—he was at the center of this in every way possible.

"We've got to get out of here." I grabbed my mother's arm with one hand and Matt's with the other.

"Harper, you are being rude," my mother protested.

"Mom, trust me on this. It's time to go."

"Sit down." There it was again. The no nonsense tone my mother could wield when necessary. I sat.

Okay, pay attention. Look around. Observe. These were the words I lived by when covering a story. This was where the nuance came from. The small details made a story richer. As uncomfortable as I felt, I thought maybe this routine would distract me long enough to sit through the rest of this seemingly endless service.

There were President Wells and Dean Ryan smiling, shaking hands, and slapping each other on the back, like the best of friends. A distinct contrast from the scene I had witnessed in the President's office. David Sharp was beaming and being congratulated, as if it had quickly been forgotten it was the death of a close family member that had made this gift possible. Everywhere I looked people were smiling and hugging. Even Matt left my side to go and interact with people I assumed to be his fellow faculty members. It was, to say the least, one of the weirdest things I had ever seen.

The minister was finally able to quiet the crowd enough to get in one last prayer of peace for the entire Sharp family before we were dismissed.

Chapter 8

The few nice restaurants in Shepperton were sure to fill up with mourners after Hank Sharp's service, so after dropping Mom off at home, still complaining I hadn't "allowed her" to stay and visit following the service, Matt and I found a hole in the wall biker bar on the outskirts of town to get a beer and commiserate.

"Okay, what the hell was that?" I asked.

"That was a lot of pressure taken off Dean Ryan and in turn, taken off of me."

"Way to look at the big picture, Matt."

"I can't help it. Earlier this week I thought my job was in danger. Now I'm working in one of the most well financed colleges on campus. It's a good thing."

"But don't you think the timing is strange? Everybody is suddenly obsessed with money and the largest donor in MCU history conveniently falls down a flight of stairs. Doesn't that strike you as odd?"

"Old people die, Harper. People with dementia wandering the halls fall downstairs sometimes. Accidents happen."

"But they shouldn't. If the security at a premiere place like Castle Woods is that lax, I'm honestly concerned about my dad's safety."

We sat sipping our beers while the requisite Lynyrd Skynyrd played on the jukebox. The tension in my shoulders was starting to ease. Matt eventually convinced me to play a game of pool.

"Did I tell you they already have a new tenant in Hank Sharp's old room?" I said, putting chalk on the end of my pool cue.

"Oh yeah? It makes me wonder who died to free up the room for your dad?"

It was hard to believe, but I hadn't even let myself think about that. Of course somebody had died making that room available for my dad. But it still didn't answer the question of why he jumped to the top of a lengthy waiting list.

I was distracted now, and Matt called me on it. "Hey, get your head in the game," he laughed. I got my head in the game long enough to beat him soundly and we ordered nachos to share as we headed back to our table. But my mind was still trying to put puzzle pieces together that, so far, didn't fit.

"So, you've alluded a couple of times to toxic tenure and having to play the politics of being a professor. If that funeral turned money-grabbing celebration wasn't toxic, then I don't know what is. I want details," I said to Matt, taking his hands and looking directly into his eyes. "I was too young and too self-absorbed to remember when my dad went up for tenure. What's this whole long, drawn-out process? Seems like being a college professor would be a super cushy job with lots of perks. Am I wrong?"

"I guess maybe that's the way it was supposed to be. But the entire landscape changed."

"Why?"

Matt sat in silence, clearly thinking about what he wanted to say.

"Harper, all I can tell you is sometimes it feels like academia is the cult that made it."

That was a bold statement.

"But if it's a cult, why didn't you get out?" I questioned, baffled by his answer.

"What else was I going to do?"

* * *

Sunday morning found me up early and headed to the Hole in One Donut Shop. I kept replaying my conversation with Matt in my mind. After much coaxing, I'd finally gotten him to open up and give me details about life as a tenure track professor. There were timelines for everything you did and if you didn't meet those timelines, you couldn't get promoted. You had to write and publish a ridiculous number of articles in well-respected journals and Matt and his other junior colleagues were responsible for teaching almost all undergraduate classes. Advising those undergraduates took up an enormous amount of time, but those duties also fell to the faculty members with the least amount of time on the job. When they did have time to focus on their own research, these early-career academics had to have the support of the dean and the tenured faculty on their research agendas, or their careers were basically over before they began. It was a minefield.

"And that son of a bitch Ryan? I hate that guy," Matt had said. "He started putting pressure on me even when I was working on my doctorate. He never liked me. Didn't think I was good enough. It's a miracle I even got this job. And you know who I have to thank for that?"

"Who?"

"Your dad. He went to bat for me. Stood toe to toe with Ryan. Told him to lay off and let me finish my dissertation. That I had ideas to contribute. I will never forget that, Harper. Of course, he paid the price for it."

"Matt, what are you talking about? You're rambling now." Knowing I had to drive us home I had stopped after two beers, but Matt had continued to drink as the afternoon wore on and his lips got looser.

"Ryan forced him out. Your dad didn't want to retire. But good old Steve Ryan, he of the fancy boots and grant writing prowess. He made Frank more and more miserable. Took classes away from him. Criticized him in public. Finally, he had no choice."

I laid in bed thinking about all Matt had shared before I had taken him to his house and put him in bed. I needed to sleep as I had the drive to Dallas to make that day, but with all this new information, my sleep had been restless at best. And if I couldn't sleep in, I might as well treat myself to the world's best donut, an ad slogan the Hole in One had been using for at least fifty years. First, I had to stop at the Wag 'n' Bag for a newspaper.

In my "real" life, I was typical of my generation and no longer even read the newspaper. Everything I needed was online. Although having grown up with a father who was a journalist, the "online argument" had driven him crazy.

"Where the hell do they think the news comes from to go online? From real journalists," he would rant. "Once they run off all the real journalists, who the hell is going to provide them with news?"

"They're called influencers," I had tried to explain.

"The way things are going, there's not going to be anybody or anything to influence."

I smiled. My father. Protector of the Fourth Estate.

But while I might not be subscribing to the daily print newspaper in Dallas, I knew in towns like Shepperton, the local newspaper was still the primary way information was communicated to its citizens. And I was betting today's newspaper would give me a great deal of insight into the mysterious Sharp family.

After arriving at the Hole in One and ordering my coffee and blueberry fritter, I settled down at a pink and turquoise table in the corner and spread the newspaper in front of me. *The Shepperton Sentinel* did not disappoint. Front page, above the fold, was a photo from yesterday's service along with almost the entire front page populated with stories on various angles of Hank Sharp's life and legacy. I wanted to read them all, but my attention was first drawn to the photo.

It was a group of people smiling and looking extremely satisfied with themselves. President Wells and Steve Ryan were cozied up next to each other. David Sharp was on the other side of the president, looking completely different than the quiet, haunted man I had found in Hank Sharp's room at Castle Woods. I read the caption to confirm to myself it was really him. David Sharp. Dr. David Sharp. Senior Vice President for Development of Murdoch Collier University. My crash course in university politics from Matt had been fascinating, but it hadn't given me much information about the role of development in the university hierarchy. I only knew this department was over all the fundraising

activities for the university. I would have to do more research. On both development and on David Sharp.

Why had he not mentioned his role at the university
when we met? Had it not come up? Was he intentionally
trying to keep something from me? And in his position, why
would he be resentful of his grandfather donating money
to MCU? Wouldn't it make his job infinitely easier? And
of course, the most troubling question of all. Had I really
heard him say "I'm glad he's dead"? Or was stress and lack
of sleep causing my mind to play tricks on me?

And for that matter, why had my mother not mentioned
who he was? She had told me some of the most personal
and tragic details of his life, but hadn't thought to mention
what he did for a living?

I was writing all of these questions down in my notebook
as fast as my hand could move. I didn't want to forget any
of them. Sitting back in my chair I took a sip of my coffee
(good, but not as good as Palace) and a bite of donut, my
thoughts swirling.

I looked at the photo again and this time noticed a young
woman standing off to the side, slightly behind the row of
smiling men. I ran my finger along the small type of the
caption again. Sophia Johnson, administrative assistant for
MCU development. She wasn't even pretending to smile. I
was afraid I really was starting to make things up in my head,
but I thought she looked... well, she looked frightened.

* * *

Something strange was going on here. Too many coincidences. Too many stories revolving around this same group

of people in a very short period. I tried to think about how I would go about getting information if this was a story I was writing. What I really needed was an inside source.

The Hole in One was starting to get busier as it got further into Sunday morning. I noticed a break in the traffic and walked up to the counter for a coffee refill.

"What do I owe you?" I asked the young man at the counter as I pulled a five-dollar bill from the front pocket of my jeans.

"Refills are on the house," he replied, filling my cup from one of the multiple pots in various stages of brewing.

I went to shove the bill back into my pocket when I noticed I had pulled out something else as well—the business card of boy reporter Nate Stinton.

"Hello, inside source."

* * *

When I got back to my parents' house, I threw my bag on the dining room table, disturbing yet another pile of papers Mom and I had been sorting the night before. My mom insisted her goal was to get all the information on this table (and shoved into her desk drawers and the metal filing cabinet in her bedroom) so organized that all the pertinent details fit on one sheet of paper. I sincerely doubted that would ever happen but figured we had to start somewhere.

I went down the hall towards my parents' room. I felt weird about calling Nate on a weekend. I felt weird about calling him at all with the way I had talked to him at the hospital. And at Old Main. So that might have to wait until tomorrow when I was back in Dallas. But in the meantime, I figured my mom might be able to fill in the blanks for me about these people connected to MCU. After all, she had been a mover and shaker in this community for years and surely knew where some additional skeletons were buried.

"Mom. Mom!" I called down the hallway.

I wasn't even remotely concerned about waking her up. She had always been an early riser and I was sure she'd probably been up for at least an hour already. But as I pushed open the bedroom door, the room was dark and still, and I could see my mother's figure on the bed.

"Mom?" I walked over to the bed and put my hand on her shoulder. "Mom?" I said more forcefully.

"Oh God." I could hear her breathing, but it was shallow and ragged. I touched her face, and it was cold to my touch. I pulled my phone from my back pocket and dialed as quickly as I could. The voice on the other end of the line finally answered.

"911. What's your emergency?"

Chapter 9

My mother was alive, thank God, but was quickly admitted to the Cardiac ICU. They spent the afternoon running what tests they could in a small, rural hospital on a Sunday. Anything in depth would have to wait until Monday. One of my first thoughts was to take her back to Dallas where she could have access to world-class medical facilities. She, of course, refused.

So instead of wrapping things up, saying my goodbyes and heading back to Dallas myself, I sat, for hours on end, in the same hospital where my journey had begun a week ago. How was that even possible? So much had happened yet so little time had passed. I felt like a different person. Older and wiser. And so tired.

I spent the night at Mom's bedside even though she had told me to go home. Honestly, I didn't want to be in the house by myself. It didn't feel right. It was hard for me to imagine I had grown up in that house. It felt completely foreign to me, particularly with neither of my parents home. Matt had called, and when I informed him of the situation had offered to bring dinner to the hospital and keep me company.

"You know I like to fly solo when times are tough," I told him.

"Yeah. I do. It's one of the things I like least about you." But he said he understood and would check in tomorrow. I was to call him immediately if I needed anything.

I ate a bag of stale Goldfish and curled my body up awkwardly into one of those hospital recliners and dozed on and off the best I could.

The bustle of Monday morning began early with Mom being whisked off for tests the nurse informed me would take a couple of hours. She suggested I go get a shower and come back around lunchtime. They might have some additional answers by then.

I was agitated and at loose ends, overwhelmingly restless. I couldn't think of anything I wanted to do. Finally, I decided I would go take a walk around campus. I had managed to avoid it all week after my doomed visit to HR. It was time. Maybe I could put some demons to rest.

When I was younger, I always enjoyed the beauty of the campus. Its familiarity and stateliness were comforting. Could I find comfort there once again? The Square had surprised me when I had opened my mind to it. Maybe MCU could do the same. I drove the short distance to campus and parked in the lot between the student union building and the library and set off through the heart of the MCU campus.

As I had hoped, being on campus did have a calming effect. It felt familiar but I also noticed new buildings, new art installations, a pond with a fountain in the middle that hadn't been here when I attended school. A complex maze of sidewalks connected every campus building and I followed the path with no particular destination. The newer buildings I didn't recognize were built in the same style of architecture as the older ones, maintaining a sense of continuity even in the face of growth and progress. Students sat under trees on picnic blankets with their laptops open, and a couple of guys with Greek fraternity letters on their t-shirts threw a frisbee in the distance. It was beautiful. I walked to the edge of the pond and tossed a couple of goldfish I found still in my pocket to the ducks swimming there. Ducks fascinated me. They were all quiet grace above the water, but I knew underneath their webbed feet were churning like crazy to maintain the illusion. I watched them for a few moments and then moved on.

All the flower beds were beautifully tended, and the grass was still green even though fall temperatures and lack of rain were turning the rest of the region brown already. I used to think a group of fairies tended to all the grass and trees and plants. Soon enough I realized a small army of real people had the job of keeping up the illusion of perfection across campus.

There was that word again. Illusion. The illusion of perfection. Was that what drove me away from this lush oasis that had for so long been so much a part of my life?

Like the grounds, maybe even like the ducks, once you understood it, so much of university life seemed like an elaborate display of smoke and mirrors. From the outside, the surface looked picturesque and ideal. It was only a chosen few that really knew what was going on behind the curtain. The more I learned about life at MCU, the more appropriate the analogy seemed to become.

The campus itself was a city within a city. Part of the surrounding community but completely separate from it at the same time. You had to have an invitation to become part of its culture whether by being accepted as a student, hired as a staff member, or appointed to faculty. You were expected to play by the rules. Matt had explained the smallest bit about the timeline by which you measure the success (or failure) of your career aspirations. The campus even had its own postal system and internal form of government that existed beyond the confines of the external community. The rules that governed the university could not be violated by its members and one had to follow the rules in order to progress upward. It was also very difficult to change your station once you had become a part of the hierarchy.

And the students, I thought, as I passed a group of them on the path circling the pond. They were so young and impressionable. They opened their hearts and their minds to the people on campus. Their parents trusted they would be well taken care of. It was an awesome burden. And for better or worse, sometimes the trust was misplaced.

The campus was still beautiful, but there was something wrong. Something strange was going on here and it was causing a knot to tighten in my stomach. So many details of life here were coming out, both good and bad, that every-thing I thought I knew was being turned upside down. What I had seen as a brief mission of mercy to help my parents was turning into something much bigger. Was I up for the task of handling it?

I was lost in my thoughts when the bell tower tolled. On most college campuses the tolling of the bells from a clock tower is how time is kept. MCU was no different. The clock tower was the centerpiece of campus and rose from the administration building as both a visual focal point and a timekeeper. The bells had always given me a sense of joy and optimism—a *Wonderful Life* kind of happiness to think somewhere angels were getting their wings each time they rang. That morning, however, they felt ominous.

Ten bells. Ten o'clock. It occurred to me I had intended to be back in Dallas at my desk by this time. Oh well. Some things seemed a little more important at the moment.

I pulled out my cell phone and the business card from my bag. Within the hour I was sitting at a table in the recesses of the Student Union Building across from Nate Stinton.

Chapter 10

"So, Ms. Fox. You've changed your mind about giving me an exclusive about your father's late-night ramblings?"

"No. Not exactly," I replied. "We're way past that."

"Tell me what's been going on. I'm sure you didn't call me just to have a cup of coffee. Or did my boyish good looks finally get to you?" He wiggled his eyebrows in what I'm sure he thought was a charming way. If the circumstances that brought me hadn't been so dire, I probably would have laughed out loud.

"I need your help," I admitted, and proceeded to tell him everything that had happened over the course of the last week, including my father's quick admission to Castle Woods, my encounters with David Sharp, and the bizarre nature of Hank Sharp's funeral. He sat quietly, listening intently.

"Have you asked yourself whose room your father got and why so quickly?" he asked. Creepy. That was the exact question Matt had asked.

"Well...I..."

"There's usually five to ten people on the waiting list at Castle Woods at any given time. I mean, you can wait six months or a year to get a room. And even if they have a room, most people can't afford it anyway."

"How do you know all that?"

"I needed a place for my grandmother a couple of years ago. She died while we were waiting."

"Oh Nate, I'm so sorry."

"No. It's okay. It is what it is."

We both sat for a moment. When it felt like a suitable length of time had passed, I finally asked, "How do we find out who had that room?"

"That's easy," he said, pulling a sleek laptop from his backpack and typing furiously at the keys. He paused and glanced up at me. "What else?"

"I want to know about David Sharp and his dad."

Nate glanced over his shoulder as if to see if anyone was close enough to hear us. "David Sharp is a world-class douchebag," he whispered.

I had to laugh at that one. "I know why I don't trust him. Why do you think he's a douchebag?"

"Aside from the fact he totally got where he is because of his family's money? He wasn't very nice to a friend of mine."

I waited but it seemed that was all Nate was going to say on the subject of David Sharp. "You said you looked at Hank Sharp's obituary in the newspaper, right?" he asked, changing the direction of the conversation.

"Yeah. I was meaning to go back and read it again but then all hell broke loose with my mom."

A file folder materialized from his backpack. He pushed it across the table towards me and said, "Take a closer look."

Nate continued his search to determine whose room my father was now occupying, and I turned my attention to Hank Sharp's obituary.

Relatively straightforward. Henry Bartholomew Sharp. Born in 1926. Military service in the Pacific during World War II. *Another member of the greatest generation lost*, I thought. Returned from the war to marry the lovely Marguerite Sharp (nee Collier) and preceded in death by his parents Henry Bartholomew Sharp, Sr. and his mother, Alice Murdoch Sharp. Graduated from MCU in 1950. Three children. Nathaniel, Cora, and Samuel. Preceded in death by his wife, Marguerite Collier Sharp, his son Samuel Sharp, and his daughter-in-law Meredith Sullivan Sharp. He is survived by blah blah blah...Lifelong devotion to Murdoch Collier University...blah blah blah...

Wait. What? My eyes went back up a few lines. Was I reading what I thought I was reading? I pulled a pen out of my bag and started sketching on the manilla folder. Could this be right? As my lines and squiggles began to take shape, I gasped, drawing Nate's attention away from his search. I looked up and he smiled knowingly, obviously aware of what I had discovered.

"What the hell?" I whispered under my breath. I glanced back at my drawing. It was a very rough sketch of a family tree.

Hank Sharp was married to a Murdoch. His mother was a Collier. I continued to add lines and names where I could. The hair on the back of my neck stood on end. Lester Murdoch and David Collier, the pioneers who had settled this area and upon whose land this university sat, were David Sharp's great-great-grandfathers. He was the living embodiment of Murdoch Collier University.

"Coincidence?" Nate wiggled his eyebrows again. "I think not."

I was stunned. And totally unprepared for what Nate said next.

"And look what I found. Your father's room was previously occupied by Louise Smith, who was found dead in her bed at Castle Woods Retirement Village on Monday morning, October tenth. I'd say probably about the same time you were begging them for a room for your dad."

"Let me see that." I pulled his computer towards me and quickly scanned the woman's obituary. Aloud I read, "Louise Smith and her husband Dexter (also formerly of Castle Woods Retirement Village) were proud, long-time donors to Murdoch Collier University."

"Want your mind blown? Click the link to ol' Dexter's obituary there at the bottom." Nate grinned knowingly.

I clicked.

"Dexter Smith, Philanthropist and Friend of MCU passes away" screamed the headline. I let my eyes again scan quickly over the obituary. In the last paragraph the words I read gave me goosebumps. "The family wishes to thank the wonderful staff at Castle Woods for taking such good care of their husband, father and grandfather. In lieu of flowers, Mr. Smith's family encourages you to make a donation in his name to Murdoch Collier University."

I looked at Nate. "You knew about this?"

"I had an inkling. There were too many people dying at Castle Woods with one other thing in common - they were donors to MCU. And I needed inside information at Castle Woods."

"And I need inside information about the university."

"I'd say you're looking at the new dynamic duo."

"How many donors have died?" I asked, unable to believe this question was coming out of my mouth.

"My research has found six donor deaths in the last three months."

"My God." I couldn't believe what I was hearing. Didn't want to believe it.

"How could this possibly be happening with no one noticing?"

"It's interesting how the system itself makes things like this possible. You know how I told you about looking for a place for my grandmother?"

I nodded.

"I did a lot of reading about nursing homes at the time. Most people don't expect their loved ones to ever come out of a nursing home. They expect them to die there. So, when somebody passes away, there's very few questions asked. Very few autopsies are performed. There's little to no regulatory oversight. People throw their hands up and say, 'Oh well'. If somebody knew how to work the system, they could easily get away with... well, they could get away with murder."

I thought about what Nate was saying. It was wrong, but it made sense. If you expected someone to die, why would you question it when it happened.

"Okay, so I understand your interest in nursing homes. But what got you interested in the development office and fundraising at MCU?"

"As so many stories go, it was about a girl," Nate replied, seemingly happy for the change in subject.

"Oh really? Tell me more."

"We met in a photojournalism class." A dreamy look came across his face. "I was a junior, and she was a senior."

"An older woman. How intriguing."

"She was so cool. She was determined. Focused. All the things I had never been. And she was obsessed with MCU."

"That seems to be a recurring theme these days."

"Yeah." He laughed. "She said she was going to be president of the university one day."

"That's ambitious. But I like somebody with a goal."

"That's what I thought too. But then she got this part time job in the development office. It was all she ever talked about. This was her ticket to the top, she said. And the more I listened to her talk, the more things didn't make sense."

"Like what?" I encouraged.

"Like, they are super secretive. They don't want anyone, and I mean anyone, to talk to potential donors. And if the donors are really wealthy, like Hank Sharp wealthy, only like two people are allowed to talk to them."

Nate continued. "The amount of control they have over the communication with these people? It struck me as weird. And the lengths they would go to wining and dining these donors to secure donations? Bizarre. Even working right in the office, she had very little access to information, and she had to shred everything. I guess I felt like there had to be more to the story and I started to dig. That's also where my belief David Sharp is a douchebag came from, by the way."

"Oh, I see." It made sense. I sat in quiet contemplation for a moment, and finally said, "What happened with you and ... what was her name?"

"Sophia. She graduated and got a promotion to a full-time position, and she didn't have time for me."

"Sophia Johnson?"

"Yeah. How did you know?"

I grabbed the newspaper and laid it out in front of us. "This Sophia Johnson?"

"Yep. That's her." Nate pointed to the frightened looking woman on the edge of the front-page photo. As I looked at the photo again, processing all I now knew, I wondered if it was fear I detected. I couldn't say this to Nate, but I also couldn't help wondering about this ambitious young woman trying to make a name for herself in the secretive world of university fundraising. Maybe the look on her face was worry. Worry she'd be discovered.

* * *

We spent the next hour passing the laptop back and forth and complementing it with searches on our respective phones. We read through the obituaries and any news coverage of the deaths of these six elderly members of our community that had been residents of Castle Woods as well as donors to MCU. In my mind I was still wondering about the possibility Sophia could be involved in all of this, but we also discovered another common thread. David Sharp.

"Look at this one. He was a pallbearer at this man's funeral," Nate pointed to the screen.

"How about this from three months ago? The headline reads 'MCU Administrator Saves the Day.' Mrs. Jewel Sanderson fell during a local charity event and guess who saved her from 'death, or at least a very severe head injury'," I quoted from *The Shepperton Sentinel* article.

"Um. Let me guess." Nate put his finger to his chin in mock thought. "David Sharp?"

"David Sharp. This guy is everywhere. Oh, and listen to this. Apparently, the incident required Mrs. Sanderson to be admitted to Castle Woods."

"I guess if you don't have enough donors to kill, you've got to start manufacturing them yourself."

"That is not funny," I said, stifling a laugh. The whole thing was so surreal you had to laugh to keep from crying at the sheer magnitude of the situation.

When we had finally exhausted all the obvious links, I sat back and sighed deeply. "So...what are we saying here?"

"I think we're saying somebody is killing off elderly donors to MCU. I also think we're saying David Sharp appears to be our prime suspect."

Chapter 11

I continued to mull over the possibility Sophia and David were in this together, and it was difficult to shake the creepy feeling I had been alone in a room with a man who was most likely a killer. And my mother thought he was a "nice young man"! But we needed more than a handful of obituaries to support our theories. Nate and I decided to divide and conquer, and each had a short list of things to investigate that afternoon. But first things first. I was starving and decided to stop by my parents' house for lunch before I began checking items off my to-do list.

Grateful we had gone to the grocery store, I pulled together stuff for a ham sandwich and added some potato chips to my plate, grabbed a Diet Dr Pepper, and cleared myself a spot at the dining table. While I was still concerned for my father's safety at Castle Woods, at least I could breathe a sigh of relief he wasn't an MCU donor. They seemed to be a population in imminent danger right now.

It was time for me to get back to the hospital to check on my mom, but I was enjoying the brief moment of peace and quiet. I shuffled through the mail I had brought in with me when I arrived. About halfway through the stack, I noticed an envelope with the MCU logo on it. Nothing unique. My parents got lots of mail from MCU. But the second line of the address made my blood run cold. It was from the MCU Office of Development.

I quickly ripped open the envelope and found inside something they referred to as a Legacy Letter. The attached correspondence (signed by David Sharp of course) informed my parents it was time for an annual update to the letter. It outlined the details of their donation, interest accrued, etc. Any updates to their giving plan were due back to the Development Office by December 1. I tried to keep reading the details of the document, but fear and anger overwhelmed me making it impossible to see straight.

* * *

"What the hell is this?" I stormed into my mother's hospital room, clutching the documents in my hand. "I only thought I was worried about Daddy before."

"Harper. You're being rude again. I have a guest."

"I honestly don't care. When were you and Daddy going to tell me you were donors to MCU?"

Mom looked over at the man who was currently occupying the one seat in the room, and they chuckled. "We were just discussing that," Mom said.

"Who the hell are you?" I asked the man, baffled by this entire scene.

"J. Johnson Laraby, Esquire. At your service," the man said, rising and coming towards me with his hand extended. I ignored it and looked back at my mother.

"Mr. Laraby is our attorney, Harper."

"Since when do we have an attorney?" I asked.

"Since your father and I had our estate plan drawn up."

"It would have been nice to know this when I was in desperate need of power of attorney papers last week."

"What on earth would you need power of attorney papers for? I'm a little under the weather, Harper. I'm not dead."

"I needed power of attorney to...oh, never mind. What is this?" I waved the offending papers at her. Sitting in the hospital parking lot, I was able to decipher the packet outlined the guidelines for the Dr. and Mrs. Frank Fox Fund for Journalistic Excellence. It further stated a large portion of their donation was accessible by the university's scholarship fund upon the death of my father. My blood had run cold.

"We'd been meaning to tell you but didn't feel it was something to discuss over the phone. We were going to wait until you made a visit. And here you are."

"Here I am," I said sarcastically. "And I thought my biggest concern for Dad was him falling down the stairs like Hank Sharp. Now this?"

"Harper, you are talking in riddles. What is going on?"

"I believe that...no, I have evidence showing ..." I could hardly get the words out of my mouth. I knew how bizarre it sounded. "...someone is killing residents at Castle Woods who are donors to MCU."

There was a moment of silence. Mom and Laraby exchanged a glance and then...they laughed. I was in fear for my father's life, and they laughed! J. Johnson Laraby, who had a small frame, wore coke-bottle glasses, and had white hair sticking up all over his head, and my mother, sitting in a hospital bed with oxygen tubes stuck up her nose, laughed. I was enraged.

"What the hell is so funny?"

"Now, Miss Fox," Laraby began. "There's no reason to get yourself all in a dither. I assure you your father is perfectly safe. Castle Woods is the most respected facility in the area, and I am certain no harm will come to any of their residents..."

"Tell that to Hank Sharp. And the six people have died at Castle Woods in the last three months. Every one of them was a donor to MCU. I think that's pretty significant. If you two want to sit around here and rewrite my mom's will or whatever the hell you are doing, have at it. I intend to save my dad's life by getting to the bottom of this."

"Harper, calm down. You've been under a great deal of stress lately. J.J. and I are making sure everything's up to date. And he brought me these beautiful flowers." She indicated a bouquet of yellow roses and baby's breath sitting on the windowsill.

"Okay. I don't know why nobody is listening to me, but I haven't got time to sit around and play tiddlywinks with you two. There's something going on here and it involves Castle Woods and MCU and I've got to do something." I was almost in tears at this point, so frustrated I could hardly put words together.

"Come here, Harper." My mom held out her hand to me and I went to her bedside.

"You need to take a breath," she said in her soothing mom voice. "Why don't you start at the beginning and tell me what's going on."

I rested my forehead on the edge of her bed, and she stroked my hair. I realized how much I had been longing for this. I didn't want to be the grown up anymore. I wanted my mom to take care of things, the way she used to.

But of course, J. Johnson Laraby had to ruin the moment. "Now, Helen, you've always said she had a fertile imagination."

I jerked my head up, the anger coursing through me again. "Oh great. You've been talking to this guy about 'my imagination' instead of telling me you and dad were donating money to MCU?"

"I told him you were extremely creative. You always were."

"This is ridiculous. I do not have time for this."

"What are you going to do?" my mom asked again.

"Why don't you sit down and tell me all about it," Laraby said, a tone in his voice as if he were talking to a small child. "If you have some legitimate concerns, I can go through the proper legal channels."

"Oh, that's a good idea. Let Mr. Laraby take care of it," my mom chimed in.

"Thanks, but no thanks. I'm going to take care of this myself, and the first thing I'm going to do is go to the police."

* * *

Soon after, I found myself back on the square, but not for sightseeing this time. The courthouse housed the offices of all law enforcement in the region, and I was going to the police.

"No, Ms. Fox. Mr. Sharp's death was purely accidental, and that is the way we are treating it," reported Bret Garrett, Chief of the Shepperton Police Department, completely dismissing my concerns. It was a feeling I was almost starting to get used to.

"You don't find it odd that a small, elderly man with dementia was able to open a heavy door locked with a security code?" I asked.

"A million different things could have happened with Mr. Sharp. It's a tragic accident," Garrett responded.

"What about the other people who have died? Every one of them were MCU donors."

"Ma'am, in Shepperton, at least half the population have a connection to MCU. It's not unusual a large portion of our elderly would be MCU donors."

"But...but..." Garrett was so calm and rational it made me question everything I had been thinking. Was I being paranoid? Was I looking for trouble where none existed? I hated it when others pointed it out, but when I was being honest with myself, my mother was right. I had always had a vivid imagination. Was I trying to avoid thinking about the reality of the situation by inventing a crime that didn't exist?

No. This was different. Something was really wrong, and I needed to trust my instincts. I took a deep breath and made up my mind I was going to stand my ground. "I would like to review the records myself and make that determination. Along with the records of each of these people who have died at Castle Woods over the last three months. The circumstances surrounding their deaths appear to be suspicious, particularly when you consider they were all donors to MCU. Look, I've got it all written down right here."

I pulled my notebook out of my bag along with a half-empty pack of chewing gum, a hairbrush, a melting string cheese, and the extra set of keys to my parents' house. All of which scattered across the floor of the police station as I tried to find the page I had written all my notes on. Finding it, I handed it to Chief Garrett.

He glanced at my scribbles in the notebook and handed it back to me.

"Listen, Ms. Fox. You've been through a lot lately and I'm sure your nerves are about shot. But these accusations simply don't have any evidence to back them up. We did not open investigations into any of these cases because there's nothing to investigate. Not to mention, no members of any of these people's families saw any reason for further investigation. And even if we had found anything even remotely suspicious about these deaths, it wouldn't be our jurisdiction. These deaths occurred on MCU property. It would be the responsibility of the campus police force to investigate."

"You've got to be kidding. Members of this community are dying mysterious deaths and you, the chief of police, aren't responsible for investigating? Unbelievable."

I thought I would try a trick I'd seen used on TV to intimidate the police into giving up critical information. I'd never had the opportunity to use it, but I was praying it might work now. "I will have my attorney, J. Johnson Laraby, get in touch and see if he can get access to any applicable records in this case. You have heard of open record laws, haven't you?"

The sheriff looked at me for a moment. *It's working*, I thought.

And then he laughed. "Why am I not surprised? Ol' J.J. got his hooks in you, huh? The guy's an ambulance chaser. A clown."

"That may be, but he's the only clown I've got in the circus at this point." I tried to muster what little dignity I could as I shoved all my belongings back into my bag and prepared to leave. As I turned the knob on the door, something occurred to me. I couldn't believe I hadn't thought of it before.

"Have you at least looked at security camera footage from Castle Woods from the night of Hank Sharp's death?" I asked.

I wasn't sure what I saw, but a glimmer of some feeling crossed Garrett's face. He rubbed his face with his hand, and I could see he was thinking about my question. Finally, he said, "I don't know why I'm telling you this, but I did ask for the security footage from Castle Woods."

"And?"

He paused again. "Their security system has been down for the last three months."

* * *

I walked out of the courthouse uncertain as to what to do next. A memory of walking up this sidewalk with my daddy to get my driver's license on the day I turned sixteen suddenly overwhelmed me.

"Oh, Daddy," I said, sinking onto the steps of the courthouse. I felt as if I couldn't move another inch. I knew I was making headway, but exhaustion swept over me. One step forward, two steps back. I wrapped my arms around my legs and rested my head on my knees. After a few quiet moments, a gentle voice said, "I believe there's a fine for loitering here. I'm not sure if you can afford the fine on an unemployed writer's salary."

I raised my eyes and looked up into Matt's sweet face. "What are you doing here?"

"I could ask you the same thing," he said, sitting down next to me. I leaned into him, placing my head on his shoulder. He wrapped his arm around me. "What's going on?"

"I was sitting here thinking that not even two weeks ago I was sitting in my apartment, minding my own business, without a care in the world. And now..." A tear rolled down my cheek. Was it the first one I had shed in the entire time I had been in Shepperton? My eyes had threatened to weep a couple of times, but this was the first all-out betrayal.

What was keeping me moving forward? Adrenaline? The need to take care of everything and everybody? How long could I go on before I completely fell apart? That was what I was most afraid of. If I let my guard down, even for a second, if I let myself feel too deeply or think too much about the situation, I would completely fall apart and be no good to anybody. I would appear weak.

I wiped the tear away.

"Now my dad is in a nursing home, my mom is in the hospital, I'm going to have to beg for my job back, residents at Castle Woods are dropping like flies and there's nothing I can do about any of it."

Matt was quiet for a long time. Finally, he said, "Yeah. Maybe you're a jinx."

For a brief moment I was devastated by Matt's remark. It was exactly the thought I was trying not to allow myself to think. Maybe I had brought all this trouble on myself somehow. But then I caught Matt smirking out of the corner of my eye and knew he was joking. I smiled a bit as well.

"Matt, I'm serious. How did I not see these things coming?"

"You haven't exactly been a frequent visitor. How could you know?"

"That's another thing. Did you know my parents hired a lawyer to help them plan their estate and create donations to MCU? I had no idea. What else is there I don't know about them? Will I ever truly understand them?"

"I'm not sure we're supposed to understand our parents. It's like trying to understand a past we aren't a part of," Matt said. "I had a history professor who said the study of history is about finding the answers to unasked questions. I took this great class on local history with him. Fascinating stuff."

"Must have been a summer session. There's not enough history in this town to fill an entire semester."

"Oh, you'd be surprised, my cynical friend. There's a lot of really cool history around here. Like this building for example."

I could tell Matt was trying to distract me from all the problems at hand. I decided to let him. "Tell me something really cool I don't know about the county courthouse."

"The story goes that when this building was being built, the mayor of the town wanted it to have the fanciest carvings of any courthouse in Texas. He hired a sculptor from Italy and brought him here to do the carvings on the cornerstones. Come look."

Matt pulled me up from the stairs and led me towards the northwest corner of the building. He pointed up to the carvings. "See those?"

"Oh yeah. They're like gargoyles or something. When I was a little girl, I thought they were totally scary."

"They are at the heart of the story, but they weren't always scary. When the sculptor arrived in town, he fell madly in love with a local Shepperton girl. He carved each of the four cornerstones to look exactly like her."

"That's bull. I've never heard that story!"

"It was one of those things nobody really wanted to put down in the history books because it took a turn for the worse."

"How? It sounds quite romantic."

"Apparently our young sculptor's love was not reciprocated and the night before his love was to marry another man right here at the courthouse, the artist came and turned each of these faces into these...gargoyle faces...and then shot himself on the steps of the courthouse."

"That's a terrible story. I can't believe I've never heard it."

"I guess it goes to show you that something that begins very beautifully can turn into something very ugly."

Matt's words hung in the air until he finally broke the spell. "How about I share a little MCU history with you over pizza tonight?" he questioned.

"I need to head over to the campus police department. After that, I think I've had enough of MCU for a while. You can't get away from it in this town." With my pity party over, I quickly switched gears. "Can you believe the police aren't even investigating Hank Sharp's death? The police chief says even if they were, it wouldn't fall under their jurisdiction. Castle Woods is on university property so it would be a campus police case."

"There you go. It's the town and gown thing. Everything is separate and everybody walks around on glass trying not to overstep each other's boundaries. It's ridiculous."

"What did you call it? Town and gown? What's that?" My journalistic curiosity kicked in, allowing me to switch gears in my head away from feeling sorry for myself and into investigative mode.

"Research shows in college towns, particularly small ones like this, a distinct division between the community itself and the academy exists. There's the town, and then there's the university - the gown - like the ones you wear for graduation. It's a common phenomenon but Shepperton has a bad case of it for sure," Matt explained.

"I was thinking about that the other day when I was on campus. Everything is separate. MCU even has its own media. Its TV station, its radio station, its social media. Hell, it even has its own newspaper. All controlled by the university administration. It makes me wonder how many things go unnoticed around here because everyone is claiming it's not their responsibility. I didn't know there was a name for it."

We had sat back down on the steps together and I rested my head on Matt's shoulder. I knew he would sit there with me forever if it was what I needed. We sighed in unison and laughed.

"Harper, what's the name of that kid from the university newspaper you've been running around with?"

"Nate. Nate Stinton. He's a good kid," I said.

"You might want to remember what you just said."

"What's that?" I had relaxed enough that my mind wasn't making connections very quickly. It was a relief.

"Administration controls university media. Think about it."

My head popped up as I realized what Matt was saying. "Do you think...?" Was Nate leading me in the direction somebody in MCU administration wanted me to go?

"I'm saying be careful who you trust."

"Good advice as always, Dr. Langley." I wanted to ponder this possibility, but I had wasted enough time today. I had responsibilities. "I appreciate the pizza offer but I think I'm going to check in on all my patients and then go get a hot bath and a good night of sleep."

Matt walked me over to where my car was parked and said, "Call me if you need anything. Anything at all."

"I promise." I kissed his cheek, threw my bag on the front seat of the car, and headed, yet again, towards campus.

Chapter 12

The Sharp donation ought to keep President Wells off my back for a while, Steve Ryan thought. Always a man of action, he gave himself the luxury of a moment to reflect, reclining in his office chair and placing his feet, housed in their custom-made designer cowboy boots, on his desk.

He had never intended to go into academia. He wanted to be a corporate raider, rich and powerful. Or so he thought. Until he became disillusioned with the corporate yes-man culture and at about the same time failed a mandatory drug test. Unsure of what direction to take he turned to graduate school. There he found a new opportunity to channel his drive and ambition. And when he discovered the concept of tenure—you could ultimately become part of a protected class with guaranteed employment for life, regardless of how aggressive you were in pursuing your goals—its achievement was all he could focus on. He was a mediocre student throughout his master's and doctoral studies but discovered he had a gift for grant writing. In academia, if you could raise money, you were a golden child, virtually untouchable. Or at least that's what he had thought until President Wells started breathing down his neck over recent fundraising failures. Hank Sharp's death had alleviated that pressure. Funny how things work out.

The usual trifecta for a new faculty member focused on the tenure track is teaching, service, and publishing. Ryan somehow managed to sidestep all the traditional requirements and focused almost solely on grant writing. He taught an occasional class, usually an introduction to communication class required for freshmen, but for the most part he focused on, and flourished, due to his grant writing skills. He was promoted quickly from assistant to associate professor and from associate to full professor at an unheard-of pace. His rise was truly meteoric. Some called him a visionary, but most found him pushy and narcissistic. This was certainly the view of the vast majority of faculty and staff in MCU's College of Media and Communication when he was named Dean. Ruling with an iron fist, the only agenda he was interested in was his own.

Ryan had an immense dislike for being questioned, particularly by know-it-all faculty members like Frank Fox. Or that kid. What was his name? Matt something. It had been fairly easy to put Frank Fox out to pasture, amping up the pressure on him until it was easier for him just to retire. He had no doubt he could do the same to Matt. He'd already begun to turn up the heat on him. Only a matter of time until he cracked under the pressure. One less problem.

The first thing that had ever really slowed Steve Ryan down was the damn heartburn that had been plaguing him for months. He had popped Tums and Rolaids like candy with very little relief. When his suit pants began to get too loose to be cinched up with a belt, he finally broke down and made an appointment with his doctor. That was two weeks ago.

The phone on his desk rang, interrupting his reflections. He answered it and listened closely to every word. All the

schooling, all the grants he had written, all the accomplishments he'd had and the awards he had won? What did they
mean now? The phone call had confirmed his worst fears.
He was dying of cancer.

Chapter 13

A brief stop by the campus police department confirmed my fear. They were not investigating Hank Sharp's death, or any of the other deaths at Castle Woods. The officer at the front desk parroted what Chief Garrett had said. It was a tragic accident. And, of course, they also claimed it would be outside their jurisdiction to investigate. If a crime such as murder had been committed, it would be up to the Shepperton Police Department or Murdoch County officials to investigate. *It's a miracle any crimes ever get solved around here*, I thought.

Honestly, I wasn't even surprised. My brief time in Shepperton had made it clear this was a "follow the rules and pass the buck" culture. Everyone in this town wanted to hide behind their rules and policies. I understood the need for guidelines, but this was excessive. How was I ever going to get to the bottom of this? Let alone keep my dad safe.

I decided to stop at the hospital next. I was feeling guilty about the way I had left things with my mother. It was time she and I had a long talk.

"Mom?" I crept as quietly as I could to her bedside.

"Hi baby," she whispered, taking my hand.

Both of us began to talk at once, our words of apology tumbling over each other. Apparently, she'd been feeling badly about the morning's events too.

"I never meant to keep you in the dark. I didn't want to bother you. You're busy living your own life," she said.

"But I'm not too busy for you or for Daddy. Why can't you understand? I want to be here for you. It's ..."

"What, Harper? What is it?"

"When I left...when I finished school..." What was I trying to say? I opted for the simplest version. "I'm sorry things went the way they did, and I haven't been around much."

Mom smiled. "You were always so independent. Even as a baby you didn't want us doing anything for you. And we had waited so long for you to come into our lives. Maybe we tried to do too much for you. Pushed you away somehow. We only ever wanted what was best for you. So, these last few years, we kind of intentionally backed off a little bit."

"Yeah. I guess I backed off too. I needed time and space."

"I'm really glad you're here now."

"Me too," I said. "Now, I don't want you to get stressed, but I do need to talk to you about something. I'm concerned for Dad's safety."

"You said something about that before. Now sit down and talk to me. Just you and me. What's going on?"

I explained, with all the details I knew, my suspicions.

"Come to think of it, there have been a lot of funerals lately. I chalked it up to old age. Funerals become your social activity when you get to a certain point in life," my mother laughed.

"That may be true, but I really believe someone is intentionally targeting these donors. And it must be someone affiliated with the university."

"I wish you wouldn't worry so much. If any of your suspicions are true, which I sincerely doubt, the small amount your father and I plan to leave MCU is a drop in the bucket compared to a donation like the one Hank Sharp made. It's hardly worth killing us over." Mom obviously wasn't taking this as seriously as I'd like. Yet I was glad to see her smile again.

Bret Garrett had made one small concession before I'd left his office earlier. He had agreed to increase the patrols around Castle Woods if it would ease my mind. He even offered to have an officer check the premises overnight. I gave Mom this bit of news, thinking it would please her, but instead she said, "Oh Harper, that's ridiculous. I'm sure the police have more important things to do than babysit an old folk's home."

"It's a retirement community."

"Whatever. You need to let this go and get some rest yourself. You're going to be in a bed right here next to me if you don't calm down."

I thought we had been making progress. But obviously, while she was at least listening to me, my mother was not taking the threat to my dad's safety seriously. I was going to have to let it go.

"I'd like someone there with Daddy."

"There's no need for you to wear yourself out. If you insist on someone staying with Frank, have Matt do it. He's stayed at the house a couple of times when your dad was being particularly difficult. Your dad adores him."

"Matt doesn't have anything better to do than babysit an old folk's home?" I laughed.

"It's a retirement community, Harper." I was relieved she was regaining her sense of humor. It was so good to laugh with her again. But once our laughter faded, I was puzzled by what she had said.

"Matt has stayed at the house? When did you all get so chummy with Matt?"

"Let me think. I suppose it was when your father was serving as his dissertation chair. They spent a great deal of time together. Matt became a bit of a fixture around the house. He was wonderful. And so helpful."

There was a new wrinkle. Yet another thing I didn't know. Why hadn't Matt mentioned he'd been spending so much time with my parents? Or that my father served as the chair of his dissertation committee?

Before I could go too far down that rabbit hole, the cardiologist appeared and confirmed Mom's diagnosis of congestive heart failure.

"It sounds worse than it is in your case, Helen. If we reduce your stress, increase your activity, and improve your diet, this can simply serve as a warning sign. Okay?"

"Okay," Mom and I said in unison. It sounded very scary and more like a death sentence than a warning. But a few more minutes of talking with the doctor and we were both convinced this was a condition that could be addressed.

"I'm going to keep you a little while longer. I want to monitor your heart function, run a stress test, and check out some other blood chemistry levels. But you should be able to go home sometime this week I would think. If you rest," the doctor concluded.

"That's my cue," I said. "I'm going to let you get some rest. I'll go check on Daddy and then relax a little myself." I kissed Mom's cheek and breathed in the sweet smell of her.

"Harper, stop worrying so much. Everything is going to be okay," she whispered.

"Yes ma'am," I replied with a smile and a squeeze of her hand. I wished I believed her.

* * *

By the time I wrapped things up with mom and left the hospital, the sun was starting to set. My mind was reeling trying to take in all the new information I'd gotten. The more I learned, the less I seemed able to see how the pieces fit together. I desperately wanted to believe everything was going to be fine, but it was impossible to shake the feeling that once the true picture emerged, it wasn't going to be a picture of a quaint little West Texas town and a mid-level university serving the needs of the region. I feared the picture that appeared would be something far darker and more dangerous.

I tried Matt's number to see if he would be willing to stay over with my dad, but the call went straight to voicemail.

The foyer at Castle Woods was bright and lovely. As I entered, I could hear classical music playing somewhere. In an alcove off the main entryway, a man was playing the piano and residents from the assisted living side of the facility were sipping wine and chatting.

"What's going on?" I asked the activities director as I passed her.

"Oh, it's our weekly happy hour. Would you like a glass of wine? Some cheese?"

"I better pass. But thank you." I continued down the hallway towards the stairs. That's what I had wanted for my parents. Wine and cheese. Classical music. Friends to play cards with. Unfortunately, that was not the hand we had been dealt.

I opened the heavy door leading to the stairwell and couldn't help but think of Hank Sharp's body being found there. I continued on to the second floor towards my father's room. Several people were wandering the hallway, one stopping me to ask if I'd seen her baby. You could hear a heated conversation between a resident and an orderly coming from another room. I usually came in the morning when it was quiet. This was a completely different world.

The medical director of the facility had told me during one of my visits about the phenomenon of Sundowning Syndrome. He explained it often occurred in patients in mid to late stages of dementia and caused patient's to be agitated, restless and even on occasion, violent or aggressive.

"Sundowning Syndrome is an insidious aspect of dementia. Most people think it's the memory loss that causes caregivers to put their loved ones in memory care, but in reality, it's the symptoms of Sundowning that wear one down until they can no longer manage care. Many dementia patients are calm throughout the day, but start exhibiting problematic behaviors as evening arrives, hence the name Sundowning. While much research has been done, no one really understands why this happens. Is it a chemical change? A fear of the dark? Who knows? Chances are your dad's wandering off that night was him demonstrating symptoms of Sundowning," Dr. Peterson explained.

"Is there anything we can do about it? Any way to treat it?" I had asked naively.

"There's a great deal of research being done on the subject. We even have a grant here at MCU allowing us to study the impact of light therapy as a treatment method. But I'm afraid we still don't really understand its root cause or the role it plays in the illnesses related to dementia. The best we can do is provide medication to calm our patients and create a safe place where they can receive good care. And, of course, hope we find an answer soon."

Seeing this phenomenon in action was definitely disturbing, and as I arrived at my father's room, even he was more agitated than normal, insisting I had taken his watch.

"Daddy, your watch is at home."

"No. I had it today. Where is my watch?"

It dawned on me his watch was missing when they found him after his late-night escapade that had first brought me to Shepperton. Was he having a distorted memory of something that had happened that night? I tried to speak in a low, calming voice. "Daddy, where do you think your watch is? I will be happy to go look for it."

"How the hell should I know? It's probably that lady down the hall. She takes stuff from everybody. She's a nutcase."

"I tell you what. Let's get ready for bed. I will see if I can find your watch and I will bring it to you."

"I want my watch."

"I understand. I will get it for you."

"Harper? How old are you?"

"I'm about to turn thirty, Daddy."

"Thirty. That's a good age."

"Yes, it is."

After much debate, I finally got Dad into his pajamas and tucked into bed. As I leaned over to kiss him on the forehead his hand shot out from underneath the covers and he grabbed my arm with so much strength it hurt a little.

"Get my watch."

I soothed him to the best of my ability and then crept out of his room on tiptoe, quietly pulling the door closed behind me. I took a deep breath and stood there for a moment, trying to get my bearings. I heard another door close farther down the hall and as I glanced towards the sound, I saw a man I had only seen twice before, but those brief glimpses had made a big impression on me. As I tried not to make a noise, he turned and headed towards the stairs at the other end of the wing.

It was Steve Ryan.

* * *

My heart was racing as, at what I thought was a safe distance, I followed Steve Ryan out of Castle Woods. I watched as he calmly got in his pickup truck and drove away. I waited until his taillights disappeared into the night before I walked to my car. As I was crossing the parking lot, my phone rang in my pocket. I didn't recognize the number. "What fresh hell is this?" I muttered under my breath.

"Hello?"

"Ms. Fox? Harper Fox?"

"Yes, this is Harper Fox."

"Um. Hi. This is David Sharp. We've met a few times over the last couple of days?"

"Yes, Mr. Sharp. I remember you." How could I forget?

"Your mother gave me your number."

Of course she did.

"I know this may sound strange, but I wanted to apologize for my behavior that day. I think I was in shock."

I struggled for something to say. This was not the phone call I was expecting.

"That's...um...certainly understandable. I appreciate you calling."

"And then at the grocery store, with your mother?"

"Yes. She can be quite talkative, can't she?"

"Well, I... um...I don't feel like you and I have had a chance to get to know each other properly. I was thinking...I was hoping ...could I buy you dinner tonight?"

"Excuse me?"

"I'm leaving the office late...and I...I'd like to buy you dinner."

"I...um..." I was at a complete loss for words. Could this day get any weirder? I had intended to follow Steve Ryan to see what he was up to. And now I was being asked out to dinner by the other prime suspect in a murder case?

"I had the pleasure of working with your father at MCU. He was a wonderful man," Sharp continued, grasping at straws to try and make this seem like a normal conversation.

"He still is," I replied.

"Yes. Yes, of course. This isn't going the way I had hoped. Maybe another night?"

From the minute I had first met this man, I had felt like he was secretive and shady. A large part of me was convinced he was involved in the deaths of not only his grandfather but also five other university donors. Furthermore, I was certain he was a direct threat to my own father. And he wanted to take me to dinner? I glanced at my watch. It was only 7:30 even though it felt like midnight. My stomach grumbled, as if on cue. And, I reminded myself, I'd been on worse blind dates. If I wanted answers, maybe talking to David Sharp was the best place to start.

"Can I meet you somewhere?" I finally answered.

"How about the Pei King on the square? Fifteen minutes?"

"I'll see you there, Mr. Sharp."

"It's Dr. Sharp. But please, call me David."

David was waiting for me at the hostess stand of the Pei King when I arrived. That first moment was one of the most awkward encounters of my life as we didn't know whether to shake hands as if we had never met or what exactly. And of course, there was the small issue that I suspected he was a killer. The awkwardness abated a little as we were led to a table next to a giant fish tank.

"I have always wondered why all Chinese restaurants have fish tanks," David said as we were being seated and handed our menus.

"I know this one," I said. "My dad spent a year abroad in Beijing when I was younger, and I asked him the same question. He told me water attracts luck and money according to feng shui. And fish always have their eyes open, so they are supposed to be able to see trouble coming."

"One of life's great mysteries finally answered," David laughed, looking at the menu.

He ordered a pupu platter for us to share and after we ordered our entrees, the mood turned somber again. "I am so sorry for being so weird that day at Castle Woods. And I'm really sorry about your dad. Dementia is not an easy thing to deal with."

"I appreciate it. I know you speak from experience." It was hard to know what to say and I figured I might as well dive right in. Nothing ventured, nothing gained. "Why didn't you tell me who you were that day?"

"Well, I don't usually lead with my job title to be honest."

"Touché."

Our conversation stalled for a few moments, but as we both let our guard down a bit, things started to flow more easily. As we were getting into the heart of the conversation, the bell on the door jingled. My seat faced the door and as I glanced up, I was surprised to see Matt walking in. He spoke briefly to the woman at the front counter and then locked eyes with me. He walked towards the table with the strangest look on his face.

"Hi, Matt. Do you know David Sharp?" I asked amiably.

"Hello, Professor," David said, offering his hand. "I don't believe I've had the pleasure."

Matt's eyes never left mine as he completely ignored David's gesture. "I thought you were too tired and too busy for dinner tonight."

"I should be home in a bubble bath," I laughed, trying to ease the tension that had suddenly taken over the room. I had never seen Matt like this in the fifteen years I had known him, and it was giving me the creeps. "But you know I can't turn down Chinese food."

"But you can turn down pizza. With me." His voice was a low monotone.

"Matt Langley?" The woman at the counter was holding a bag of take out. Matt turned, took the bag, and walked out into the night without another word.

"That was weird," David said.

"Everything that has happened to me lately has been weird," I agreed. "Will you excuse me for a minute?" I couldn't let Matt leave like that.

I ran out the door as Matt crossed the square. "Matt," I called to him. "Matt!"

I caught up to him under one of the restored streetlights lighting the square. "What is wrong with you?"

"What is wrong with you? You turn me down for dinner for the one millionth time in the time we've known each other and go out to dinner with that guy."

"Matt, it just happened this way. I'm trying to get information from him. I think he could be involved in Hank Sharp's death."

"You looked awfully cozy in there to be doing investigative journalism."

"That is exactly what I was doing. But honestly, I really don't owe you an explanation."

"No, Harper, you don't owe me an explanation. And I don't owe you or your family any more of my time and devotion either. Go enjoy your date with David Sharp." He turned and walked away.

"Matt, it's not a date," I called after him. "I am trying to figure out this case. I am trying to protect my dad." He kept walking.

Eventually I turned back towards the Pei King with a heaviness in my heart. It wasn't the first time Matt and I had ever argued. And come to think of it, our arguments were usually about somebody I was dating. But this wasn't a date! I really was trying to get information. The bells on the door jingled as I reentered.

"Everything all right?" David asked, genuine concern in his eyes.

"Fine. Now, where were we?"

We talked for over an hour enjoying our family style kung pao chicken and phoenix and dragon. At one point, I got an embarrassingly long noodle from our side dish of lo mein. Not knowing what else to do, I had to slurp it into my mouth. I was only mildly embarrassed by the puckered up kissy face and accompanying noise I had to make to get the thing into my mouth until David said, "Harper, not on the first date."

Then I was completely embarrassed and felt the front of my neck growing red and hot. While some people blush, I turn bright red from the neck up. I finally managed to respond, "This is not a date."

"I know. I'm kidding," David said.

And while it wasn't a date, David really was quite charming. I had to keep reminding myself he had most likely killed six people for their money. Eventually, over a pot of hot tea and fortune cookies, we began talking about growing up in the shadow of the great Murdoch Collier University.

"I almost felt like MCU was the favorite child and I was an afterthought," David said.

"My mom mentioned Mr. Sharp was actually your grandfather."

"Yes, that's true. But my real father died when I was so young that Hank was the only dad I ever knew. It was always easier to call him my dad than explain the whole long, drawn-out story."

"I understand. And honestly, I felt the same way. My dad was always focused on his students and there wasn't much room for me," I added. "So why did you stay here and go to work for the university?"

"I ask myself that question all the time. Guilt I guess. My older brother and sister got out. They went away to school and got on with their lives. But my parents, I mean my grandparents, particularly my granddad, talked all the time about his legacy. Who would continue the legacy?"

"Yeah, especially when you're a direct descendent of the founders." The minute the words were out of my mouth, I knew I had screwed up. Damn Chinese beer. I had let my guard down.

"How did you know that?" The warm conversation instantly turned cold.

"I...um..." Think Harper. Think! Figuring the truth was better than a lie I said, "When I read your dad's obituary. It was right there. I made the connection."

David relaxed a little. "Oh. I don't share that information with many people. It comes with a lot of baggage. People assume I am only where I am because of my family ties. But the truth is, I probably worked harder to prove myself than somebody else would have."

The tense moment abated, but the open conversation we had been having was clearly over. I was kicking myself for accidentally playing a card I intended to keep close to my vest, and David suddenly seemed distracted.

"Check please," he mouthed to the waitress.

"This was great," he said as we walked out into the night. "I'm sorry if I caused any problems with your boyfriend."

"Matt? He's not my boyfriend. He's an old friend who apparently is feeling a little possessive of my time while I'm in town."

"While you're in town? You're not staying in Shepperton? I thought perhaps with your dad's situation...and your mom..." I had also shared more about my own circumstances with David than I intended. I could get this back on track though.

"No. As soon as I get things settled here, I'm heading back to Dallas. I've already screwed up one assignment. I've got to try and keep the tatters of my writing career together."

"Couldn't you write from here? Technology has made the world smaller and smaller."

"I guess I could. I just do better at a bit of a distance from Shepperton."

"I certainly understand that. Harper, thanks so much for giving me a chance to explain myself and to get to know you a little better. I hope I can see you again before you escape the shackles of MCU."

We both laughed uncomfortably.

"It was a pleasure, Harper Fox." He stuck his hand out.

I took it. "The pleasure was mine, David Sharp."

As I walked to my car, I felt the extra fortune cookie I had put in the pocket of my jacket. I popped it open, sticking half of it in my mouth.

The fortune read, "An upset is an opportunity to see the truth."

* * *

When I got to my parents' house, I was so tired I fell face first onto the bed, fully clothed. I was awakened by the sound of my phone buzzing next to my hand. I was disoriented by the daylight peeking through the curtains. What time was it?

"Harper?" It was Nate Stinton. "They found another person dead in their bed at Castle Woods this morning."

"Wait. What?" I sat up, trying to process what Nate was saying. Someone else had died overnight. Was it a dream? I knew it wasn't. "Oh my God Nate, he was there last night. Dean Ryan was at Castle Woods."

For a moment, I thought about what Matt had said about Nate and the university's control over the newspaper. But there came a point where I had to trust my instincts and every fiber of my being believed Nate was following the story where it was leading. It might bite me in the end, but I trusted Nate. He was the one person who was doing what he was doing for all the right reasons. Well, there was one other person I knew I could trust.

As I was throwing on a pair of jeans and pulling my hair into a ponytail, I tried Matt's number. No answer. Voicemail. "Matt, I am so sorry about last night. It was a big misunderstanding. Please call me back! Not only is your dean an asshole. He's also a killer."

Chapter 14

Within thirty minutes, Nate and I were back at our corner table in the SUB. The SUB, short for student union building, was another element most universities shared. A central location in which to meet, eat, or study, different universities called it different things, but for those of us at MCU, it was the SUB. Fast food restaurants lined the walls, coffee flowed freely at more than one location, and lounge chairs were arranged in front of a big screen TV, usually showing news or a sporting event. Tables and chairs hosted groups of students, studying or sharing the latest campus gossip. It was fairly easily to get lost in the crowd at the SUB, but due to the delicate nature of our discussions, Nate and I had gravitated to a table out of the mainstream.

With his laptop between us, we had a document open and were listing all the information we had with no detail being too small.

"How did you find out about the death at Castle Woods?" I asked as Nate drew lines between the list of victims on the left and our suspects on the right.

"I have a police scanner. I heard the call go out this morning."

"You are a dork."

"I'm a dork who's going to solve this case," Nate said with pride.

"Oh my God. I forgot to tell you. Did you know the video surveillance system at Castle Woods has been down for the same amount of time as these deaths have been occurring?"

"That's huge. Where did you get that little detail and when were you going to tell me?"

"Chief Garrett told me yesterday. About the same time he told me there was no way he was going to investigate these deaths as murders."

"But don't you get it? That should narrow our list of suspects down to only those people who would know there was no video surveillance. The murders began when someone knew they were far less likely to get caught."

"Hmm. I wonder if Steve Ryan would know. Like...was it discussed in meetings he would have attended or something? It makes so much sense it would be Ryan. If you follow the money, he's the one benefiting the most from all these deaths. His college gets this influx of funds and he's off the hook to continue to do as he pleases."

"Yeah. It really does make sense," Nate said, continuing to type. He finally paused. "But I still see David Sharp as the most likely suspect. Dean Ryan has an awful lot to lose."

"And David Sharp doesn't?"

"I see your point, but..." Nate was looking at the screen, obviously deep in thought. "What time did you see Ryan at Castle Woods?"

I tried to think back to the series of events last night. "It had to be about seven thirty. That's when David called me to have dinner."

"David?"

"Yes, David. David Sharp. He wanted to explain why he'd been acting so strangely."

"What did he say? 'Sorry about my behavior. I've been distracted with all this killing'? Again, let me ask when you were going to share this juicy little tidbit? Oh yeah, and what the hell were you doing having dinner with David Sharp?"

"I'm getting tired of being given the third degree about who I have dinner with!"

"Okay, okay." Nate put his hands up in surrender. "I think that detail might be important to this investigation. But let's think about this. If you saw Dean Ryan at seven thirty, he is most likely not responsible for this death."

"How do you figure that?"

"They do vitals checks around ten thirty each night before they have a shift change at eleven. This patient had to still be alive then."

"I don't even want to know why you know all that."

"I'm a helluva a journalist," he said, a twinkle in his eye. "What time did you and lover boy finish dinner?"

While Nate had grown on me over the last couple of days, he was still as annoying as the first day I'd met him. "Dr. Sharp and I finished dinner at about ten forty-five."

"Making your new lover available at the right time to knock off our latest victim. He probably still has the code to the doors from visiting his dad. He's a familiar face around Castle Woods and probably wouldn't attract the attention of the staff. Easy in. Twist of the oxygen cord. And he's home before he turns into a pumpkin at midnight."

"No. No way. It can't be him. And we don't even know at this point if this even is another murder. This person could have died of natural causes."

"Harper, nobody's dying of natural causes these days."

At that moment I looked up and was shocked to see Matt navigating the maze of tables towards where Nate and I were sitting. His face was intense, and I was worried his anger last night had carried over into today. But as he grew closer, I could see his face soften.

"Harper, are you okay?" he said, totally like the Matt I knew and loved. Relief swept over me as I flung my arms around his neck.

"Yes, I'm okay. And I'm so sorry about last night. It was all a big misunderstanding. I..."

"No, I'm the one that should be apologizing. I was a total jerk last night and I had no right to..."

"Mmm hmm." Nate cleared his throat. "Excuse me? We've got several murders to solve here."

"Oh yes. Matt, this is Nate Stinton from the *MCU Mirror*. Nate, this is Dr. Matt Langley. My oldest and dearest friend."

The two shook hands and Matt pulled another chair up to the table.

"Start at the beginning. What is this about Dean Ryan being a murderer? I mean, I hate the guy, but I don't think he's a killer."

"He was there. Last night. He was at Castle Woods. And then this morning there was another person dead," I explained.

"I hate to burst your bubble, but I know why Dean Ryan was at Castle Woods last night," Matt said.

Nate and I both looked at him questioningly.

"He was there to visit his sister. Rumor has it he goes almost every night. She is his one soft spot. She suffers from early onset dementia. He had her moved to Castle Woods a couple of months ago so she would be close by, and he could be more involved in her care."

I was momentarily stumped, but then a realization dawned on me. "A couple of months ago was when the murders started. And he's the one reaping the benefits of these donations. Not to mention, visiting his sick sister seems awfully touchy feely for such a jerk."

"I know on *Murder She Wrote* things wrap up nicely like that, but that's not the real world," Matt said with a chuckle. I punched his arm. "Oh, and add this to your little spreadsheet over there." Matt gestured at Nate's laptop. There was tension between the two I didn't understand. "President Wells issued a statement this morning that, effective immediately, Steve Ryan is stepping down from his role as dean."

"What? Why?" I asked.

"No idea. But I'm sure I'll know as soon as I get to my office. News spreads like wildfire around here," Matt said matter-of-factly. "So what do you guys know? It's time we get to the bottom of this. Enough is enough already." Matt's presence, and his willingness to help, calmed my nerves.

We started at the beginning and laid out the information as clearly as we could, hoping Matt would see the connections as clearly as we did. I even shared my concern Sophia Johnson might be involved although Nate took great offense at my suggestion.

"She would never do anything that would hurt MCU," Nate argued.

"If you look at it from another viewpoint, it could be seen as helping MCU. This financial crisis is impacting universities all over the country. What better way to ease the pressure than to have an influx of new donor money?" Matt reasoned.

"Do you want to take it outside Langley? Sophia had nothing to do with this." I had never seen Nate angry before, but Matt's level head kept things from getting out of hand.

"Calm down. I'm not saying your girlfriend's a serial killer. I'm saying money can be a strong motivator." Nate relaxed a bit and we continued to analyze all the angles we were aware of. It was nice to have Matt bring a fresh set of eyes to the situation.

A phone buzzed and we all checked our devices. It was Nate's.

"You're not going to believe this," he said, passing his phone across the table so Matt and I could see his screen. It was an invitation to a reception and check presentation for Hank Sharp's donation.

"I guess I know where we'll be tomorrow at three," I said. We agreed the reception would give us an opportunity to see all the major players in one room together. It could be very telling.

Matt and Nate both had classes to go to and we were packing up our stuff when another phone buzzing caused us to check our pockets. It was mine this time. It was a nurse's assistant at Castle Woods informing me my father was particularly agitated today and could I please come immediately to try and calm him down.

"I'm on my way."

I ran to my car and found yet another yellow ticket on my windshield. I ripped it off, jumped in my car and sped the few blocks to Castle Woods. But upon my arrival, Dad appeared quite calm and was tucked into a recliner in the corner of his room watching a game show on the small television we had purchased for him. Seated next to him was the same person who had informed me of Hank Sharp's passing. I had only seen her a couple of times during my visits to Castle Woods.

She rose. "Ms. Fox. I am sorry to bring you here under false pretenses, but I had to talk to you."

"My father is okay?"

"He's fine. He's having a good morning. Right, Mr. Frank?"

My dad grumbled but his eyes never left the television.

"I'm confused. What do you need to talk to me about?" I asked.

She walked over and closed the door to my father's room and then leaned in close to me as she said, "I'm afraid for your father's safety."

Chapter 15

"Okay, you've got my attention. I'm all ears," I replied.

"I didn't know who else to go to. I can't lose my job. But there's something strange going on around here. Mr. Frank is such a sweetheart. And then I saw you here the morning they found Mr. Sharp and you were so nice." Her name tag read Shelby, and she was clearly nervous and rambling. I needed her to calm down and focus. I slowly, gently took her hand in mine.

"Shelby, I'm so glad you reached out. What's going on?"

"I mostly work nights, or I would have called you sooner. This is a rare day shift for me."

"Okay." I intentionally kept my voice low so as not to startle her. I looked encouragingly into her eyes.

"Too many people have died lately," she finally said.

"Yes, I think so too. What do you think is happening?"

"I know this may sound crazy, but I think someone is killing them," she whispered.

"Do you have any idea who?"

"I have no idea. But I have been trying to keep my eyes open around here. I needed to tell somebody so they could tell me what to do."

"What makes you think these deaths aren't from natural causes? Or in Mr. Sharp's case, an accident?"

"Please don't tell anyone I told you this. I need this job. I've got three kids at home."

"I won't tell anyone unless I absolutely have to, and I will try to leave your name out of it." It wasn't much of a promise, but it was the best I could do under the circumstances.

Shelby glanced around as if to see if anyone was listening. My dad was still engrossed in whatever show was on his TV. "When someone passes away at night, part of my responsibility is to clean up their body and their room so we can put a new patient in as soon as possible. Then I write up a report about the circumstances of their death."

"Okay."

"Dr. Peterson makes the final call on time of death and stuff like that."

"Peterson is here in the middle of the night to do that?" I asked.

"No, that's just it. He does it based on what I put in my write-up. And I don't want that kind of responsibility. I'm not even an actual nurse - yet." It was obvious these protocols had been weighing on her, and I agreed she shouldn't be put in that kind of position. But I could see there was more she wanted to say. Finally, she continued. "With these last several deaths, I noticed strange little things - things I'd never seen before."

"Like what?" Could this be the smoking gun I was looking for? Come on Shelby.

"Take Ms. Smith for example. She was in this room before your daddy moved in."

"Right. I knew that." I was consciously trying to assure Shelby she wasn't spilling all the beans.

"She was a diabetic. Took insulin regularly. And when she passed, and I was straightening up her room, I noticed two empty bottles of insulin in the trash. She had been given two doses that night."

"By who?"

"Her records were incomplete. No note as to who gave her the doses."

"That's weird."

"That's what I thought. And then there was Mrs. Parks. She was a doozy. Always wore full makeup. Even when she went to bed. When I went to her room the night she died there was a pillow on the floor, over on the far side of her bed. You know how you sometimes knock a pillow off in the night?"

I nodded gently, trying to keep my face and demeanor as calm as possible out of fear she'd leave before sharing all she knew. Inside, however, I was screaming, "Get to the point, Shelby!"

"It had her lipstick on it. Like it had been held over her face."

"Oh my God." I had to make a concerted effort to keep breathing normally and keep my face from revealing the shock I was feeling. The last thing I wanted to do was scare Shelby away.

"Mr. Wester's oxygen tank was disconnected," she continued.

Wester, I thought. Yes, he was one of the patients on my list who was also an MCU donor.

"Some small things about these last several resident deaths that seemed off, at least to me," Shelby said.

"These aren't that small. These things are extremely suspicious. And you haven't told anyone about this?"

"Well, not exactly. I was afraid of getting in trouble. I try to do my job and go home. I did put notes in each one of my reports, but I don't know for a fact anybody ever read them. Or if they did, they didn't want details. Nobody has ever said anything to me about it."

"Do you mind if I take notes?" I pulled my notebook from my bag, but Shelby shook her head. She was getting nervous.

"I've been gone too long already. I need to get back to work." With that, she stood from where we'd been sitting on the edge of my father's bed, asked Dad if he needed anything, and headed towards the door. She paused. "One more thing."

"Yes?"

"You know how every resident has a picture and something about themselves outside their door?"

"Yes." That job had fallen to me when we moved Dad in. To put together his "Get to Know Me" sheet hanging outside his door. It was supposed to give visitors an idea of something they could talk about with each resident. I had found myself reading them myself when I came to visit. So many fascinating people with amazing stories now lived here and their accomplishments had been boiled down to a single sheet of paper taped to the wall in a memory care facility. "What about them?"

"I read them. Every person who died was connected to MCU. That's why I was worried about your daddy." She quickly and quietly closed the door behind her and was gone.

It wasn't my imagination, and Nate and I hadn't exaggerated the connection. Matt saw it. Shelby saw it. And it was so clear even an outsider with no affiliation to the university could see the pattern, and the strange circumstances that surrounded each death. The truth was becoming clearer.

I had no idea what to do next. Should I call the police? Call Nate? Did this woman's observations prove anything? My journalistic training kicked in and told me I needed someone to corroborate this information. But who?

Finally, it dawned on me. If this ordeal was a circus, Annette Smith was the ringleader. If something was amiss here at Castle Woods, she would almost have to know about it.

"Daddy, I've got to go." I kissed his cheek. "It's almost lunchtime. And I think I'm going to come over and spend the night with you tonight. We can have a slumber party. How 'bout that?"

"Sure. That'd be nice. But only if my show is over," he replied.

"Of course! I wouldn't dream of interfering with your show. I'll see you later."

I rode the elevator down to the lobby, trying to figure out what I was going to say to Annette Smith. Did I try to charm her into giving me information or did I confront her and see if she would break? I knew I should call either Nate or Matt, or maybe even Bret Garrett, to join me. But I didn't want the momentum of the moment to get away. If Annette was involved, surely she couldn't, or at least, wouldn't do anything to me in her office in broad daylight. It seemed like the most logical explanation that this was an inside job at Castle Woods. Someone who knew their way around. Someone who knew about the surveillance system. Someone with the codes to open and close all the doors. But why would someone at Castle Woods care about donors to MCU? Yes, Castle Woods was on the MCU campus and technically a part of its health care training program, but it wasn't getting any funding from the donors who had died. All the donor money was going to the College of Media and Communication. Wasn't it?

I had made that assumption. I had been so focused on my dad's position, Matt's new position, and Dean Ryan all being affiliated with the College of Media and Communication I had blinders on. Then, of course, there had been Hank Sharp's enormous gift to them. I had focused on that one connection entirely. I knew better than that and could kick myself. This could be the break we needed.

I went over to a far corner of the lobby and called Nate.

"Can you find out what department on campus each of the dead donor's money was going to?" I whispered.

"It's all going to Media and Comms, right?"

"I thought the same thing, but now I'm not so sure. Would you look into it, please? Is any of the money going directly to Castle Woods? I'll call you back in a bit."

They had hired a new clerk at the front desk, an insipid girl named Julie.

"I need to see Annette Smith," I informed her as I walked behind the counter and knocked on Annette's door. What was that noise coming from her office?

"Uh, you can't go in there," Julie said in her monotone voice.

"Watch me." I swung open the door to Annette's office and caught her huddled over a paper shredder. Only it wasn't Annette Smith at all. A tall Hispanic woman rose from behind Annette's desk and held her hand out to me.

"I don't believe we've had the pleasure." Her voice was like butter. "I'm Monica Moralez, Vice President of AgeStage International."

"Where is Annette? What are you doing here?"

"Ms. Smith has been relieved of her duties here at Castle Woods. I'm here doing the final audit in my organization's purchase of the property. I'll be running things until we can find a suitable replacement. And you are?"

"Harper. Harper Fox." All of my bravado and eagerness to confront Annette had withered. I didn't know what to say in the face of this new development.

"Ah, Ms. Fox. Your father Frank is a guest with us. Correct?"

"Um, yes. Yes, he is. But..."

"I can assure you his level of care will only improve under the auspices of AgeStage management. I'm afraid the university had gotten a bit lax in its practices over the years."

"But..." Come on Harper. Use your words. "Why would MCU sell out to a big corporation? And why now?"

"This buyout has been in the works for a long time, Ms. Fox. And I assure you, it is mutually beneficial both to my organization and to MCU. They have funds now to put into other, more strategic initiatives, and we have the opportunity to expand into a region we find to be very attractive."

Money. Funding. It was a recurring theme. How did it all go together? This woman was smooth. No doubt about that. Too smooth actually, and I found myself wishing Annette Smith was back at her desk. Monica Moralez felt intimidating.

I was lost in my own thoughts when Monica said, "Can I help you with something, Ms. Fox? I have a great deal to do to sort through the mess I've been left with." She motioned to all the papers strewn haphazardly across the desk. It dawned on me she must have just arrived. And Annette Smith had just left. The coffee mug from Royale Annette always had with her was still sitting on the desk. I didn't believe for a second this was the preplanned audit Monica Moralez was playing it down to be.

I steeled myself.

"Call me Harper. I had been meaning to ask Annette who was in my father's room before it became available." Perhaps this would allow me to gauge whether she would tell me the truth. "We...um...found a couple of things when we were moving my dad in, and we wanted to make sure we got them back to the family."

"Oh, I would have to refer back to the records on that, Ms. Fox. Could we make an appointment for one day next week? And if you don't mind...I..." She motioned again to her desk. At that moment, the radio unit in its charger on the windowsill crackled to life.

"Guard to base. Come in base."

Monica rolled her eyes and let out a sigh of irritation, the first chink I had seen in her armor. She held up one finger indicating I should give her a minute. Picking up the radio she said in a harsh tone, "This is base. Go ahead."

"We've got an issue here at the southeast stairwell. The lock on the door is broken and..."

Monica quickly cut off the security guard mid-sentence. "I'll be right there. Now Ms. Fox..."

"The southeast stairwell, huh? Have you had a chance to review the records about Hank Sharp falling to his death in the southeast stairwell? I'm no lawyer, but a broken lock sounds like grounds for a lawsuit to me."

"I assure you this is a new problem that had absolutely nothing to do with Hank Sharp's death. Ms. Fox, I'm going to have to ask you to leave now."

She did know about it. Just what was being covered up with this AgeStage takeover? And by whom?

I was thrilled I had managed to fluster this seemingly unflappable woman, and I wasn't going to stop now. "If you could confirm for me my father's room was previously the room of Louise Smith, I will get out of your hair. Oh wait, I do have another question I need to ask you. It's a billing question. My mother is quite concerned."

Between gritted teeth, Monica said, "Yes, that sounds right. I believe that was Mrs. Smith's room. Now please leave."

I wasn't going anywhere. "I really don't mind waiting so we can discuss that billing question."

"Oh, all right. Wait here." She bustled off angrily.

She had left her door open, but when I was sure she was out of earshot, I peeked out the door. Julie was nowhere to be seen. I went quickly over to the large desk and ruffled my hands over the papers there. They were innocuous enough. Mostly bills from vendors for food, a recent air conditioning repair, and a handwritten invoice from a banjo player who had entertained the residents last month. Off to the edge of the desk I noticed a notebook with the AgeStage logo on the cover. Underneath the logo were the words Acquisition Protocols. I flipped the notebook open, certain Monica would return any second and catch me snooping. But the first page was all I needed to see. It was contact information for what were listed as Project Partners. MCU contact? I didn't want to believe it. David Sharp.

Chapter 16

The sun had long since set, but Sophia Johnson was still at her desk poring over the numbers one last time. All the annual reports to donors and copies of their legacy letters for updating had gone out on time. But the numbers weren't adding up. If each of the donors came through with their expected donations, they would still come up tens of thousands of dollars short, not only of their annual goal, but also meeting last year's numbers. And that was a big if. There was always some attrition expected. But why weren't people giving their usual donations? They were far enough removed from the 2008 recession for that to be figured into the equation. The housing market was stable. Unemployment rates were high but improving. All economic indicators pointed to donors' confidence increasing so they could stand to invest a little money in a good cause—especially for a big tax break. If she were able to calculate in the large gifts they'd recently received, that would more than make up for the shortfall. But for reasons she did not understand, she had been given a clear directive not to include those monies.

"Hey babe," came a voice from the darkened lobby of the development offices.

"Hey. You scared me," she replied, quickly shuffling the papers she was reviewing into a nearby notebook and shoving it to the side of her desk. "I was just getting ready to wrap up for the evening."

"Why don't we order some Chinese and have it delivered to my place?" the man said, coming up behind Sophia and placing his hands on her shoulders, ostensibly for a neck rub.

"Sounds good. Let me get my things together and I'll meet you there."

"I don't mind waiting for a few minutes. That way I can walk you to your car. I don't want you out alone after dark."

He ran a finger along a row of notebooks in the bookcase that took up one entire wall of Sophia's office as she pulled her wallet and lipstick from her desk drawer and put them into her bag. The notebooks went from floor to ceiling and were arranged alphabetically by the last name of the donor. He was looking for one specific notebook. D – E – F. Fanning. Franklin. Damnit! It wasn't there. Where the hell could it be?

"Okay. I'm ready," Sophia said as she slung her backpack over her shoulder. Old student habits were hard to break. "What are you hungry for tonight? I think I may get the beef and broccoli."

She took his arm as they walked out of the office and into the night towards the parking lot.

Chapter 17

They were releasing Mom from the hospital Friday around noon, so I spent a large portion of Thursday cleaning up around the house preparing for her return. I didn't want her to have any additional stress. I swept all the paperwork from the dining table into a cardboard box to deal with later and put clean sheets on all the beds. Laundry was done, towels were folded, and I looked around with a sense of satisfaction. It was short-lived.

A text message from Matt buzzed on my phone. "Ryan=Cancer," it said.

I sat down in one of the overstuffed leather chairs in the living room to think about the ramifications of this. On one hand, I was saddened anybody would have to suffer through cancer. On the other hand, what was more dangerous than a man with nothing to lose? Everything seemed to point to David Sharp being responsible for the deaths at Castle Woods. And yet, every piece of new information seemed to complicate things even further. Ryan could still be guilty.

Yes, I was stubborn. But I wasn't stupid. It was time to ask for help.

I showered and dressed for the reception, leaving myself plenty of time to make one stop before I met Matt and

Nate. As I entered the police station there was a small part of me that was vain enough to be pleased when Bret Garrett looked up from his desk and said, "Why, Ms. Fox. You clean up nicely."

"Have you got a minute?" I asked.

"I'm all yours," he said.

Over the course of the next twenty minutes, I laid it all out, every last detail. Garrett jotted a few notes on the blotter on his desk and asked a couple of questions, but for the most part, it was a rambling monologue of everything that had happened over the last week and a half. I wasn't sure if he thought I'd lost my grip on reality or if I was making a compelling argument, but I knew I had to tell someone. I'd done everything I could. Nate had done everything he could. We needed help.

At long last I finished my story. Garrett leaned back in his desk chair and looked at the ceiling for a moment. Leaning forward towards me he asked, "So where are you going now? The reception on campus?"

"Yes, I'm supposed to meet Matt and Nate there in a few minutes."

"I'm going with you." He rose from his desk and reached for the cowboy hat hanging on a coat rack in the corner of his office. Some might think the cowboy hats that were standard issue with the Shepperton police uniform were cliche. But I had to admit that on Bret Garrett, the look suited him.

"Oh, I don't think that's a good idea. Who knows who'll be at this reception? You might tip off the killer."

"Harper, at this point, if there is a killer, I think it's high time we do tip them off, don't you?"

I couldn't argue with that.

"I'll stay in the background to keep an eye on things. You won't even know I'm there," Garrett assured me, as we walked towards our cars. "Act normal."

I was relieved to see Matt and Nate waiting outside of the Alumni Pavilion for me so we could all walk in together. I was nervous and sweating a little by the time I reached them even though a welcome cold front had finally blown in some fall temperatures the night before.

"Are you okay?" they said in unison as I approached.

"I'm better now," I said, taking each of them by the arm. With these two by my side, I knew I could handle anything that might be coming.

As they did for most parties, MCU had pulled out all the stops for the reception. Gold and blue balloon arches graced each entrance, and a mustang ice sculpture was the centerpiece of the table covered with lavish hors d'oeuvres. I wished my mom could have been there. She would have loved the bacon wrapped shrimp. Waiters with trays of champagne meandered through the crowd. I desperately wanted a glass but figured I'd better keep my wits about me. News crews from the local media and the bigger cities in the region were set up in one corner. Someone had thought of every detail.

My eyes roamed the crowd. There was Steve Ryan. Based on what I had learned of the man, I guessed even cancer couldn't stop him from one last moment of glory. President Wells was moving through the crowd, shaking hands and laughing loudly. And there was David. He had everything in the world going for him. Money. Good looks. Influence. Had none of it been enough? Had greed turned him into a monster? Over David's shoulder I saw Bret Garrett unobtrusively enter the room through a side door. True to his word, he was hardly noticeable as President Wells approached the podium to begin his remarks.

Nate leaned over and whispered in my ear, "There's Sophia. Isn't she beautiful?"

She was indeed. Dressed in a royal blue dress with matching heels, she stood off to the side of the room, alert and ready to take action at a moment's notice if something was needed. I was certain she had planned and executed every detail of this party. But as was her job, she let others take all the credit and soak up every bit of the spotlight.

And Nate. He was so no-nonsense. Sharp and witty. Always focused. I thought back to that first day when he had barged into my dad's hospital room to get a story. But today, he looked like a lost puppy as he stole glances Sophia's way.

The speeches were brief and filled with self-congratulatory bravado. And there it was. The big Publisher's Clearing House type check. David Sharp presented it to President Wells as the crowd cheered. Ten million dollars from the estate of Henry Bartholomew Sharp.

As the official presentation concluded, each of the major players went off to be interviewed by various members of the media and the partygoers had their champagne glasses refilled. Matt was talking to a few of his colleagues, and I noticed Nate inching closer to where Sophia was standing. I caught his eye and mouthed the words, "Go talk to her," as I made my way towards the hors d'oeuvres table to see if there were any shrimp left. As I added a few cubes of cheese to my plate, a voice behind me said, "So, we meet again." It was David.

"Great party," I said, able to think of nothing more interesting than that under the circumstances.

"Yes. It's a great day for MCU," he said, with no genuine enthusiasm in his voice.

Before David could say anything else, Bret Garrett had appeared at his side. "Mr. Sharp. I'd like you to come with me."

"What is this about?" David responded.

"I'd like to ask you a few questions regarding the recent deaths at Castle Woods. It won't take long."

"Can't you see I'm in the middle of an event here? I can't talk to you now."

Bret put his hand underneath David's elbow and said, "Yes, and it's a lovely event. I'm sure you don't want to make a scene right in the middle of it, do you? If you come with me quietly, we can get this all sorted out in no time."

I couldn't tell if David was embarrassed or angry or what exactly, but he wouldn't make eye contact with me as he walked out the far exit next to the chief of police. Matt and Nate were at my side immediately.

"What the hell was that?" Nate asked.

"What's going on?" Matt added.

"I told Garrett everything. I had to," I admitted. "This was so much bigger than what the three of us could handle. I guess Garrett felt like there was enough information to question David Sharp about the murders."

"Wow. This is one of the best MCU parties I've ever been to," Nate laughed.

"Absolutely. I think this calls for a toast!" Matt said, flagging down one of the waiters and grabbing three glasses of champagne. "Here's to... Murdoch Collier University."

"Here's to MCU." Nate and I clinked glasses.

The mild-mannered reception took on a life of its own as the afternoon turned into evening. It seemed as long as the champagne was flowing, guests were unwilling to call it a night. But at last, the crowd started to thin, and Nate announced he had a test he needed to study for the next day.

"Well, I guess it's just you and me, kid," Matt grinned. "Hey. You still owe me that pizza. Why don't you come over for a while and relax? I think you've earned it. Hey, and look. I've got beverages!" He pulled a bottle of champagne from inside his jacket. "A buddy of mine working the event gave it to me. Said there was plenty."

I was hungry, having only had four bacon wrapped shrimp and a couple of cheese cubes all day. What the hell. I'd be back on nurse duty when my mom got out of the hospital. Why not enjoy tonight?

With pizza delivered and our shoes tossed aside, Matt and I sat on the floor of the living room in his bungalow. We were eating the pizza right out of the box and sipping the last of the champagne out of coffee mugs. "I wonder what David Sharp is up to right now?" he laughed.

I didn't find Matt's comment funny and realized I was feeling a little bit sorry for David. Escorted from an event of such personal and professional significance by the police. And I knew the reason it had happened was because of me. My mood soured. But Matt, having had way too much to drink, wasn't picking up on my change in temperament, and kept talking.

"So. What are you going to do now, Harper?" he asked, slurring my name slightly.

"Well, I've got an apartment full of dead houseplants to get back to," I said sarcastically.

"You could stay here and get a job on campus. Our university marketing office could use somebody like you."

"Absolutely not. I would never work at MCU." I was simply stating a fact. And I knew under other circumstances Matt would have understood that. But with God only knows how much champagne in him, Matt took obvious offense at my words. Never try to have a serious conversation with a drunk. The thought crossed my mind perhaps Matt had developed a drinking problem. This was the second time in just a few days I'd seen him have way too much to drink. I'd keep my eye on the situation and talk to him about it if it continued to be an issue.

"What is your problem with MCU? What has your problem always been with MCU?" Matt raised his voice in anger.

"I don't have a problem with MCU. I just don't want to work here."

"You've always acted like you were too good for this place," Matt continued, as if I hadn't said anything. "What the hell is wrong with you?"

"Matt, I'm going to go before we say things we don't mean." I started to get up, but Matt grabbed my arm and pulled me back down on the floor beside him. I jerked my arm from his grip and backed away, ready to act immediately if it became necessary.

"I like it here, Harper. No, I love it here. I went other places. But you know what? Nowhere felt like this. Like home. Why do you have to be rich or famous to have a good life? Why do you have to live in New York or Los Angeles to be happy? You don't! Your dad knew that. We talked about it. He knew he could go back out there somewhere and be part of the rat race. But your dad knew even if you won the rat race, you were still a rat."

With that, Matt seemed to run out of steam.

"I'm sorry, Harper. I still can't hold my alcohol."

I laughed uncomfortably, still a bit wary. "You never could." We both leaned back and rested our heads on the couch.

"You know what, Matt. You're right."

"About what?"

"About everything. You know what I've learned during my time here in Shepperton?"

"What's that?"

"I've learned everybody has to define success and happiness for themselves. They have to determine where home is for themselves. I'm jealous as hell of the people who found it here. And I wish I could be one of them. I just don't know if I can. But you know what else I've learned?"

"Hmmm?" Matt mumbled.

"I've learned I want to come back and visit a lot more often."

I looked over at Matt, looking forward to seeing his joy at my introspection and personal growth.

He was sound asleep.

* * *

As soundly and dreamlessly as I slept, I awoke with a start, confused as to where I was or what time it was. It was still dark outside. Oh yes, I had fallen asleep on Matt's couch. Of course. I had pulled a blanket over him and put a pillow under his head the night before and crashed.

My phone sat out of reach on the coffee table. I retrieved it and it said 5:04 a.m. My stomach rolled with a slight bit of champagne induced nausea. I needed to get home and get ready to pick up my mom, but it was far too early to wake up Matt. I was certain he was going to have a massive hangover. I decided to get my stuff together and leave him a note I'd call him later.

I crawled gingerly off the couch and being as quiet as possible, I slipped on my shoes and slung my bag over my shoulder. Pen and paper? I padded over to Matt's desk that was strangely neat for a working academic based on my experience with my dad. There was no paper or pen for a note on the desk's surface. I pulled open the middle drawer.

Time stood still. I was frozen in place and the gears in my brain began to grind. Scenes from the last two weeks played in rapid succession. In the drawer was a watch that looked exactly like my father's. I picked it up and turned it over to look at the back. "Happy Retirement. Love Helen and Harper" was engraved on the back.

"What are you doing?"

I jumped and dropped the watch back in the drawer, slamming it shut.

"I was looking for a piece of paper so I could leave you a note." I tried to sound normal and slow my breathing. "I've got to get home and get my Florence Nightingale outfit on."

"Let's have some coffee. I'll make you breakfast." Matt groaned as he got up and moved towards me. He kissed my cheek.

"I've really got to go. I'll call you later."

Chapter 18

At some point, Nate had given me his home address, but up to then, I'd never needed it. Now I searched through the notes on my phone and headed towards his on-campus apartment complex. I took the stairs two at a time and began banging on his door.

"Can I help you?" The door finally opened slightly, and I saw an obviously sleepy Sophia Johnson wearing a shirt I recognized as Nate's. If I hadn't been in such a panic, I'd have been proud of the guy, but there was no time for that now.

"What the hell, Harper? It's not even six o'clock yet," Nate said, putting on a shirt as he met me at the door.

"It's Matt. Oh my God. I can't believe I'm saying this. David Sharp didn't do anything. It's been Matt all along."

"Wait, what?"

I quickly ran through the details that had once been murky but were now so clear. Then I said, "There's one thing I need to ask you. Remember when I first came to town, and you came to the hospital wanting a story about my dad?"

Nate nodded.

"How did you know he was missing that night? Was it your police scanner?" I was truly hoping that it was.

"No. I was...busy that night." He scratched his head, both trying to wake up and think back. "I turned it off. I got a phone call from an anonymous source that tipped me off."

"That's what I was afraid of." I pulled out my phone and began to dial.

Bret Garrett had given me his cell phone number in case of an emergency with either of my parents. I never would have believed I would need to call him for this. I finished dialing his number.

"Harper, are you sure about this?" Garrett asked when I told him why I was calling.

"I'm positive. We had it all wrong."

"Then I need to put out an APB for Dr. Matt Langley."

"No, you don't need to do that. I know exactly where he is."

* * *

As I suspected, in the time it had taken me to get to Nate's and contact Garrett, Matt had gone to the place I knew he would be. He was sitting on the steps of the court-house. I walked towards him, surprisingly calm. I knew it would be a matter of minutes before Chief Garrett showed up, probably with guns blazing, to arrest Matt. We didn't have much time.

"Hey," I said.

"Hey," he replied. "You found the watch."

"Yeah. I did. I know you lured my dad out of the house and called in the anonymous tip to Nate. But Matt, I'm only going to ask you this once and I want you to tell me the truth. Did you really kill all those other people?"

He hung his head.

"They wouldn't have wanted to live that way. You know that," he finally said.

"That is not for you to decide, Matt."

"They were worth more to MCU dead than alive. They all wanted to make a difference at the university."

My God. I was beginning to realize how truly sick Matt was.

"And my father?"

"I never would have hurt your dad. You have to believe that. He was my mentor. I ..." he paused. "I wanted you to come home. I knew if he went missing, even for a little while, your heart wouldn't let you stay away. I never would have hurt your dad," he repeated, almost as if he was trying to convince himself. "I wanted to get you back to town. I knew once you were here, you'd see what we could have."

"Did you lure him out of the house that night?" I asked. Matt nodded. "And you called Nate with an anonymous tip?" He again nodded in the affirmative. "Why did you take the watch and the wallet?" I felt stupid asking such trivial questions, but looking back, I can only assume I was trying to apply logic to a completely incomprehensible situation.

"I don't know," he whispered. "I guess I thought it would make it more believable. Man, he loved that watch."

"Oh, Matt." Finally, the tears began to flow as I sat on the steps next to this man whom I had cared about for most of my life. How had I not seen how broken he had become?

Matt's eyes had taken on an almost wild look as he said, "I was going to have everything I ever wanted. I was going to be a professor at MCU. You'd come back to town and realize you belonged here. That you belonged with me. We'd live happily ever after. But no. You're out running around with David Sharp and some kid from the newspaper. You wouldn't stop digging." He was getting angry now. I hoped Bret Garrett would be here soon.

"That damn Nate Stinton. He's been stirring up trouble since the day he walked on this campus. He won't follow the rules. He thinks he's so smart. I knew he'd keep digging. But I didn't think you would. I thought you'd take care of your mom and dad and see what life could be like here."

"But why hurt the people at Castle Woods?"

"It was like this perfect storm. The Royale asked if I'd like to make a few bucks doing the deliveries at Castle Woods. They gave me total access to come in and out as I pleased, all the door codes. Then I met Sophia..."

"Sophia Johnson? In the development office? She was in on this?"

"Oh God no. She was a sweet girl trying to make her way in this shitty business. She was easy enough to charm."

Every word he said ripped my heart out, but I needed him to keep talking. I needed to understand. "So you met Sophia?" I encouraged.

"Sometimes I'd go hang out with her in the development office. I'd grade papers while she ran her reports. And then she'd leave me alone with all those notebooks filled with donor reports. It was all right there. It was easy to find out who was at Castle Woods and whose donations would immediately benefit the college. Ryan was riding my ass. He'd hated me since graduate school. Tried to undermine me every way he could. All he could think about was money. I kept searching for a way to get him to shut up and leave me alone."

"That must have been awful, Matt." I was rubbing his back gently. Where was Bret Garrett? I'd told Nate, who had insisted on coming with me, to stay in the car no matter what. But I wasn't sure how much longer I could keep this up.

"And then there was the answer," Matt continued. "Castle Woods was shorthanded. Nobody was reading the reports or paying any attention to what was going on. Families didn't request autopsies because people were expected to die in that place. They died of being old and in some ways, it was a relief to the families. No one was watching."

"The pressure. You can't imagine," he was ranting now and getting increasingly agitated. "Write grants. Find money. No research assistants for you Mr. Assistant Professor. I could see the writing on the wall. I finally got here. This place I worked so hard for. I couldn't lose it because of money. Those people were dying anyway. Living this miserable existence. I really did them a favor. And I took the financial pressure off the college. I didn't mind being an unsung hero. I wanted the freedom to do my job."

"A hero? Matt, this is crazy." My patience was wearing thin.

"Yeah. I know. It all made sense at the time. I wanted you and my life at MCU. That's all I ever wanted."

Two police cars, blue and red lights flashing, careened around opposite corners onto the square and pulled up in front of the courthouse. Garrett and another officer whose name I could never remember, jumped from the cars with their guns pointed directly towards where Matt and I were seated.

"Even things that start out beautiful can turn ugly," Matt whispered as the officers moved towards us and took Matt into custody.

Chapter 19

Several weeks passed and I found myself still in Shepperton.

My mom had been released from the hospital and we were enjoying spending time together. I knew she needed a hobby - something that would keep her occupied but also be relaxing and low stress. Inspiration had hit me as I was driving by the Hobby Barn one day. I went in and picked out a beautiful assortment of yarn and a variety pack of crochet hooks. My grandmother, Mom's mom, had taught me how to crochet when I was a little girl. My mom had been too busy then, raising me and being a big shot businesswoman. "I don't have the patience for that," she had insisted at the time. But I took to it like a duck to water and had continued to fall back on the needlework as a stress reliever even into adulthood. I decided it was high time I taught mom. As October rolled into November, we started a routine of brewing an afternoon pot of tea and enjoying a cup as we snuggled up in her bed together and I taught her the simplest of stitches.

"You loop it and then pull it through. You don't pull it through and then loop it," I said, pointing at the stitches she was trying to make with her burgundy yarn on one of the first afternoons of our crochet lessons.

"I'm looping, I'm looping," she said with a smile. She eventually started to get the hang of it.

She had taken her cardiologist's words to heart and didn't let things bother her nearly as much as she had in the past. She went for a walk each morning, and we were experimenting with cooking vegetarian dishes. She was still convinced cottage cheese and cantaloupe was the breakfast of champions, but she was expanding her horizons.

It turned out the AgeStage takeover at Castle Woods was in no way nefarious. The timing was one of those strange coincidences and it had been in the works for a long time - actually a couple of years - just as the news blurb I'd found early on in my research had said. The trend to have teaching hospitals affiliated with universities was apparently a difficult model to maintain. Regulations, insurance issues, and of course, funding, were better handled by the large corporations who specialized in care for the elderly. I was glad to hear through the grapevine Castle Woods intended to continue a close partnership with MCU and to provide innovative opportunities for its students. Even Monica Moralez turned out to not be so bad. As mom and I continued to visit Daddy regularly, Monica and I got to know each other better. She was ambitious, but she was kind. She just wasn't much in the personality department. We had agreed to get together for lunch sometime soon.

Neither Dr. Peterson nor Shelby were found guilty of any wrongdoing. Sadly, they had been cogs in a broken wheel. Peterson left Castle Woods eventually and opened a family medical practice in another small West Texas town. Shelby applied and was accepted to MCU's nursing program where she received a full scholarship. To my knowledge, no one knew what had ever happened to Annette Smith.

Daddy's condition didn't improve, but it also hadn't worsened. Mom and I picked him up on Sunday afternoons, had lunch together, and took him to campus to feed the ducks. He continued to beat me regularly at Trivial Pursuit.

Within six weeks of his diagnosis with esophageal cancer, Steve Ryan was dead. His sister Beverly passed not long after. A small, private service was held in their memory.

And me? I found I didn't miss *Dallas Alice* at all, so my leave of absence became permanent, and I was looking at subletting my apartment for the last few months of my lease.

The best news? The night I had gone to Castle Woods and found all the residents so agitated had led me to a deep interest in Sundowning Syndrome. I researched at length and found some time to write a feature length article on it, weaving the science and research in with tales of my fascinating father, Professor Frank Fox. A national magazine had bought the article for a respectable sum, enough to keep me afloat while I figured out my next move. And that very afternoon, the editor had called me to discuss the possibility of turning the article into a book.

I had immediately called Jose Taquero and reserved a table for a large group. I messaged my new circle of friends and shared the news along with the invitation to join me for dinner around six.

Nate and Sophia were the first to arrive. I was looking forward to some good conversation, but they were too busy looking dreamily into each other's eyes. My mom arrived shortly thereafter and was extremely irritated when I instructed our server she was not to have too much salt. "So will you please put sugar on the rim of my margarita?" she asked, looking my way as if daring me to say anything.

"Yes ma'am," the server replied as I rolled my eyes.

"Lighten up, Harper," my mom said, pulling up the chair next to mine.

Kyle Baxter and his wife, Amanda, along with their adorable two-year-old Nathan came in with Tristan. Tristan busied herself getting a highchair for the toddler, while Kyle came and kissed my mother and I both on the cheek.

"How are you feeling, Helen?" he inquired.

"Great! I'm fixing to be the mother of a published author."

As everyone was getting settled and placing their drink orders, I was disappointed to see David Sharp hadn't accepted the invitation I had left as a message on his voicemail. I could understand though. He'd been through a lot. I'd put him through a lot. Maybe he'd come around eventually.

As I looked around the table, I couldn't help but be saddened Matt wasn't there. No matter how devastated I was to uncover what he had done, I wondered, and not for the first time, if the university itself didn't have some culpability in his downfall. Dean Ryan had targeted him for no reason and the field of academia was a pressure cooker. It was a wonder anybody survived it. Matt had finally been on the path to finding himself, yet the scrutiny and the expectations were so intense. Was there a place where a young tenure track professor could flourish? He had felt like the only problem he could solve was the problem of money. What he did was horrible and inexcusable. But my heart broke for him a little bit anyway. And I missed him.

Matt's attorney was working on a defense of not guilty by reason of insanity and assured me Matt was likely to get the care he needed. Our best hope was a sentence at the North Texas State Hospital in Vernon. Six miles from the

Oklahoma border, it was a fully accredited psychiatric hospital that would hopefully be able to help heal his brilliant mind that had become so clouded. It was also close enough I could visit.

Margaritas flowed and laughter filled the air. I was delighted when Chief Garrett strolled into the restaurant and pulled a chair up at the far end of the table. He ordered a Corona and helped himself to the chips and salsa.

"You can't drink on the job, Chief Garrett," I teased.

"I am off duty, Ms. Fox. And I cannot turn down an invitation for Mexican food." Kyle's baby, Nathan, was getting restless, and Chief Garrett pulled him from his highchair and began bouncing him on his knee.

I was feeling very pleased with myself for pulling together this diverse group of friends and family and assumed our party was at last complete, but as our entrees were being delivered, the last person I had thought to invite appeared.

"Hello President Wells," I called, drawing his attention to our table.

"Hello everybody! I'm not going to intrude on your party. I'm just going to grab a quick bite with my wife, but I wanted to come over and say hello," he said to the group. He shook hands and kissed cheeks around the table. He then kneeled down between my mother and me and said more quietly, "I wanted you both to know we've set up a scholarship in our Journalism department in Frank's honor. I hope it will honor his legacy and relieve some of the pressure on our graduate students, so we don't see a repeat of this tragedy."

"Joe, that is amazing," my mother said, a tear rolling down her cheek. "Frank will be so honored. I will tell him when I see him tomorrow."

"Great. You give him my best," he said. "How is his room at Castle Woods, by the way?" He smiled and winked at my mother.

It had been the one question I had yet to find an answer to. How my father had skipped the waiting list to get a room at Castle Woods so quickly.

"It was you? You got him the room?" I said in disbelief.

"What's the point of being president if you can't pull a few strings now and then." He turned to leave and then turned back towards where I was seated at the head of the table. "Harper, if you ever want to join the MCU family in some capacity, we could sure use somebody like you. You might even want to think about going to graduate school. You could take advantage of that scholarship one day," he said.

"Oh, I don't think so, Dr. Wells. But thank you."

With a knowing look on his face, he smiled.

"Never say never, Harper Fox."

Acknowledgments

I have always enjoyed reading the acknowledgements of other authors and have looked forward to the day I would have the opportunity to write my own! There are so many people to thank!

Thank you to Anna Hatton and Elizabeth Nettleton who were willing to read early drafts of this work and provided great insights. Penni Askew, my wonderful editor, whose praise kept me writing and whose critiques made my writing better. Robert Stein, my favorite millennial, and the person responsible for the name and much of the character of Nate Stinton. And to Brianne van Reenen, Founder and Curator of Wild Lark Books. Her vision for a place where authors are recognized and supported as artists, has brought light and literature to our little corner of the world. I look forward to many more adventures with you!

I must also thank my wonderful family. I am a very lucky mom to have children who are also artists and understand the ups and downs that go with a project of this size. And to Malcolm Brownell, PhD., who likened the writing of this book to completing a dissertation. Thanks, Dr. Brownell. I love you.

Lauren Cassel Brownell has written for magazines in the United States and Canada, served as a food columnist for one of Florida's largest newspapers, written two short plays that have both been produced by local community theatres, and is the author of *Zen and the Art of Housekeeping: The Path to Finding Meaning in Your Cleaning.*

She has been an advertising and marketing executive in a variety of industries and currently serves as Director of Marketing and Communication for Texas Tech University's College of Education. She lives in Lubbock, Texas with her family.

CPSIA information can be obtained
at www.ICGtesting.com
Printed in the USA
BVHW032357270822
645664BV00005B/20